I knew you needed time to find your own way,

and I prayed, daily, that it would lead you to me."

NEVER *Dance*
with a DUKE

Seductive Scoundrels Book 7

COLLETTE CAMERON

Blue Rose Romance®
Portland, Oregon

Sweet-to-Spicy Timeless Romance®

NEVER DANCE WITH A DUKE
Seductive Scoundrels
Copyright © 2020 Collette Cameron®
Cover Design by Kim Killion

Attn: Permissions Coordinator
Blue Rose Romance®
8420 N Ivanhoe St. #83054
Portland, Oregon 97203

eBook ISBN: 9781954307643
Print Book ISBN: 9781954307650

www.collettecameron.com

Seductive Scoundrels
A Diamond for a Duke
Only a Duke Would Dare
A December with a Duke
What Would a Duke Do?
Wooed by a Wicked Duke
Duchess of His Heart
Never Dance with a Duke
Earl of Wainthorpe
Earl of Scarborough
Wedding her Christmas Duke
The Debutante and the Duke
Earl of Keyworth

Coming soon in the series!
How to Win A Duke's Heart
Loved by a Dangerous Duke
When a Duke Loves a Lass

Check out Collette's Other Series

Daughters of Desire (Scandalous Ladies)
Highland Heather Romancing a Scot
The Blue Rose Regency Romances:
The Culpepper Misses
Castle Brides
The Honorable Rogues®
Heart of a Scot

Collections

Lords in Love
The Honorable Rogues® Books 1-3
The Honorable Rogues® Books 4-6
Seductive Scoundrels Series Books 1-3
Seductive Scoundrels Series Books 4-6
The Blue Rose Regency Romances-
The Culpepper Misses Series 1-2

Dedication

For everyone who enjoys early morning walks as much as Nicolette and I do.

Hyde Park, London
Morning, 15 May 1810

Nicolette Twistleton puffed out a soft, poignant sigh as she strolled the sun-dappled footpath along the southern bank of the Serpentine in Hyde Park.

Bella, her pug puppy, frolicked about, yanking on her leash in an energetic attempt to investigate every single thing she happened upon: leaves, sticks, insects, rocks, worms, people— and their shoes. She had a particular penchant for the latter, which she thoroughly enjoyed ruining with her needle-like teeth.

Thus far, a trio of Nicolette's slippers and a pair of half-boots had met a gruesome end.

A pair of brownish-gray mourning doves swooped across the pathway, landing beneath a flowering cherry tree's heavily laden branches. Cooing softly, they touched bills, in what almost appeared to be an avian kiss.

Several feet behind Nicolette—enough to permit a bit of privacy but not so much as to cause raised eyebrows—her maid, Jane, carried Nicolette's parasol and hummed softly to herself.

A distracted half-smile curving her mouth, Jane twirled the plump pink peony she'd plucked from the front flower bed when they left the house an hour ago.

Jane was madly in love.

She and Jack, one of the Twistleton grooms, were to wed next month. Her dreamy expression and wistful sighs were beginning to wear on Nicolette's tattered nerves, however. As happy as she was for the loyal servant, she couldn't prevent the reoccurring twinge in the region of her heart.

Oh, the pang most assuredly was *not* envy.

No indeed—God forbid such a wholly ludicrous idea.

The familiar ache was a bitter reminder of Nicolette's absolute humiliation and devastation two years ago. Her then betrothed, Alfonse Bremerton, the Duke of Kilbourne, had jilted her a mere four hours before they were to have exchanged vows at St. George's Church. After the odious churl had danced with her thrice at a ball the night before, pretending to be the doting soon-to-be groom.

When his note had arrived the morn of their wedding day, she'd eagerly opened it, expecting a love note.

Nicolette,
I cannot marry you.
Forgive me.
K

Kilbourne hadn't even deemed her worthy of an endearment.

Seven words.

Twelve short syllables.

Thirteen if you counted Alfonse's initial, which she did not.

That was all it took to destroy Nicolette's life, her plans for the future, and make her determined never to trust a rogue again. Or even marry for that matter.

How could she possibly ever trust her gullible heart again?

By the time she'd received her former betrothed's cryptic note calling off their wedding, the cowardly cur was already half-way to Gretna Green with Maribelle Grosenick—a vulgarly rich heiress hailing from America.

Even more mortifying—salt in an already festering wound—Kilbourne's heir, a healthy male child, had entered the world a mere six-and one-half months later. Irrefutable proof that the blackguard had been playing Nicolette false during their courtship.

And he'd dared—*dared, by God*!—to plead with her to consummate their vows the eve of their wedding. After all, they were to exchange vows on the morrow, he'd cajoled, and all the while, Kilbourne had been plotting to scorn her.

Scapegrace. Hog-grubber. Jackanape.

Typical man—controlled by that *thing* between his legs and not the brain in the head atop his shoulders. And most assuredly not governed by any sense of decency, honor, or chivalry.

"Contemptible, maggot-patted bounder." She snorted, loudly and most indelicately, earning her a curious look from Bella's big brown eyes and also sending the cooing doves to wing.

"No, I wasn't talking to you, my precious darling," Nicolette told the sweet little dog, she acquired the purebred pug in Colechester two months ago. Bending, she patted Bella's soft head, earning a doggy grin in return. "Are you having fun?"

Tongue lolling, Bella gazed at her adoringly and promptly tried to nip Nicolette's gloved fingers in an attempt to play. Everything was a chew toy for the teething pup.

Thank goodness for this little dog who'd helped ease the sadness and loneliness Nicolette hid from the world behind a carefully constructed contradictory facade: part carefree flirt and part coldly aloof spinster.

She donned her mask of gay coquette and pretended to all of the world that she didn't have a single care. That being jilted hadn't affected her in the least. Until a man became too familiar or forward, then she retreated into an icy shell.

Men never knew which she'd be, on any given occasion, and she preferred it that way. It kept them slightly off-balance, which meant they couldn't ever get close to her. And if they couldn't get close, she ran no risk of heartbreak again.

It also kept the gentlemen from presuming too much. And Nicolette's caustic tongue deterred even the more daring of the bucks from over boldness. She'd once overheard two matrons declaring Nicolette's tongue was sharp enough to scrape barnacles from a ship.

Bah, she scolded herself for allowing her mind to wander down these melancholy paths on such a lovely day.

She *was* better off without Kilbourne.

That, she now knew to be an unqualified fact. For

a man who'd stray while betrothed would assuredly do so once vows had been exchanged.

Had Maribelle considered that when she'd dallied with another's affianced?

She ought to have.

For if the rumors were accurate—and there was generally a tidbit of truth in all tattle if one dug around enough to find the nugget—he'd recently become romantically entangled with an Italian opera singer.

Another sound of disgust echoed in Nicolette's throat.

That made his fifth mistress since marrying.

Perchance, the lure of a title had sufficed for Maribelle, and after providing the requisite heir, she was content with her lot. Gossip also had it that the Duchess of Kilbourne was in the Americas for an *extensive* visit.

So perhaps, she'd come to her senses, after all.

Nevertheless, from that fateful day onward, at twenty years old, Nicolette had relegated love and all of the other flimflam associated with the useless emotion to a fusty, secluded corner of her heart.

Where, in time, she hoped to forget she'd ever entertained such foolish, fanciful notions.

Pragmatism had replaced romanticism—reality instead of girlish daydreams.

Her desire for love had been exchanged with a passion for adventure. At least that's what she believed this restlessness besetting her was. She'd approached Mama and Ansley about the possibility of traveling to exotic foreign destinations. But both had looked at her with such incredulity, she might've sprouted a pair of wings upon her shoulders or feathers in her hair.

Her mother and brother *did not* share her enthusiasm for exploring other cultures and places. They were perfectly content dividing their time between London during the Season and Fawtonbrooke Hall the rest of the time.

Oh, an occasional short holiday to Bath or Bristol, or even a jaunt to France or Scotland for a few days, *might* be acceptable. But nothing so dramatic or distant as exploring ancient cities or other antiquities.

However, for a spinster facing a boring, *lonely* future, the notion of visiting faraway, mystical places had taken the place of her desire for love, marriage, and children.

Or so Nicolette told herself. Repeatedly. Daily.

However, as contradictory as it might be, she was sincerely glad for her married friends. Several had recently fallen in love and were happy as grigs with their very own dukes. Just because love hadn't worked out well for her, didn't mean she begrudged them their happily ever afters.

She, alone, seemed to have been Cupid's failure.

Puzzling her forehead, she bit her lower lip and skirted a fallen branch, a remnant from last night's windstorm.

The whole being jilted ordeal still hurt. Awfully. Encompassed Nicolette with a desolation, she only acknowledged when lying in her lonely bed at night. When all of the day's activities were behind her, and her mind was, at last, permitted to contemplate the reality she stoically ignored otherwise.

Nicolette faced a solitary and purposeless future, and when she'd grown tired of proving to *le beau monde* that she didn't care about being tossed aside, what would she do?

Upon spying a twig on the path, Bella yipped and tugged upon her leash. She pounced on her unwitting prey before clamping her little jaws around the eight-inch long stick and marching along proudly for a few steps, her curled tail in the air.

Only in the last couple of weeks had Nicolette's training Bella to walk on a leash met with enough success that the puppy could accompany her the entire length of her morning walks.

When an immense long-haired black dog loped by on the adjacent green, she promptly deserted her toy, dropping it to the pathway and trying with all of her might to chase the dog. The runt of her litter, Bella had no notion of her extra small size, even at almost four months old.

In the distance, an impatient male voice called after the large dog. "Sampson! Stop."

Oh, dear. Had he escaped his owner?

Undoubtedly, and one snap of his big jaws would severely injure Bella.

"No, Bella," Nicolette gently admonished.

The biscuit-colored pup was still learning appropriate leash behavior. She strained against her restraint, her sturdy little body visibly quivering for another moment before Bella reluctantly resumed her version of strolling.

These early morning promenades, when Mama was still abed, were the only times Nicolette claimed for herself. She raised her face to catch a ray of sun feathering through the bright green foliage.

Its warmth soothed and rejuvenated her.

It was a glorious spring morning, and she breathed out a deep, cleansing breath.

Typically, the weather would've invigorated Nicolette and helped prepare her to face whatever social fracas Mama had decided she must endure for the day and evening.

Always—*always, dash it all*—with the ultimate goal of seeing her happily wed. Mama wasn't ready to quit the field just yet regarding Nicolette's nuptials—*more's the pity*. She still dreamed her only daughter would find a suitable husband and eventual contentment.

And live *happily ever after*.

Pshaw. Nicolette wrinkled her nose.

As if that was ever going to happen now.

She'd given love a chance once, and with a few exceptions—her brother Ansley, Earl of Scarborough, being one—she'd henceforth concluded men were toads. No, toads could be cute, intriguing creatures, and it was unfair to make the comparison.

Surely she could do better than that.

Cockroaches.

Yes, men were cockroaches—the lot of them.

Most especially handsome dukes.

Well, excluding her friends' husbands—the Dukes of Sheffield, Sutcliffe, Bainbridge, and Pennington— who were decent enough chaps, she supposed.

Fine then, not *all* lords were devil's spawns. Just most.

Mindful of her propensity to freckle, Nicolette lowered her face, and her pink bonnet's brim blocked the soothing sunshine once more. A smile tipped her mouth as Bella spotted a squirrel and made to charge after the small creature.

However, this particular squirrel, nearly as big as the pug, wasn't having any of Bella's bravado. It sat upon its haunches, scolding the puppy soundly for her impudence.

"*Ruff.*" Bella hopped on all fours. "*Ruff. Ruff. Ruff.*"

Hop. Hop. Hop.

She bounced on her sturdy little legs again, whining fretfully in her attempts to reach the taunting rodent.

Why, the little gray wretch appeared to grin tauntingly at Bella. It's small, sharp, yellow teeth clearly showing, it even made little chirping noises, which sounded distinctly like squirrely chuckles.

The dog that had raced by earlier must've heard Bella's frantic barks for it came tearing across the green straight toward them. Nicolette's heart faltered before kicking into double time.

A liveried footman charged after the creature, but he couldn't possibly catch the animal before he was upon Nicolette.

Good Lord!

Was the enormous beast friendly?

She wasn't waiting to find out.

She'd just scooped Bella into her arms when the rambunctious, hairy dog plowed into her. Panting and drooling, it reared onto its hind legs.

Heaven's above!

Releasing a startled squeak, Nicolette staggered under the creature's weight. Resting his enormous paws on Nicolette's arms, all the while rooting about with his broad muzzle, the brute tried to sniff Bella.

"Miss Nicolette!" Jane screamed, dropping her flower and rushing forward, wielding the parasol like a saber. She whacked the mongrel on his haunches, but she might as well have used a feather for all the good it did.

"Get away from them!" she cried.

Thwack.

"Leave her be, you great, hairy brute!" Jane ordered.

Thwack. Thwack.

Nicolette well knew Jane didn't possess the gumption to strike the dog hard enough to hurt it. Not that it would feel much through the thick pelt covering its large frame.

Her heart stampeding and Bella growling a warning low in her throat, Nicolette wrapped her arms more securely about the outraged, wriggling puppy. Shoulders hunched, she turned her back to the other dog, still persisting in trying to snuffle Bella.

Why must dogs always greet one another with intrusive, and sometimes rather embarrassing, sniffing?

Nicolette feared that at any moment, she'd feel sharp teeth shredding her flesh or hear Bella shriek in pain.

What manner of owner permitted their dog—a dog *this* large and intimidating—to run wild in Hyde Park for pity's sake? In truth, the circumstance might send a woman with a less robust constitution into histrionics or a swoon.

Nicolette wasn't prone to either. She wasn't that sort of woman and didn't plan on becoming one.

The dog hadn't growled or bared its teeth, and therefore, she deduced it wasn't vicious. But the sheer size of the beast made standing upright almost impossible. Under the creature's weight, Nicolette stumbled forward a pair of steps. It certainly felt as if the dog weighed almost as much as she.

A shrill whistle rent the air a fraction before a stern male voice ordered, "Sampson. Down."

Sniffing loudly and giving one last determined lunge toward Bella cradled in Nicolette's embrace, the dog succeeded in knocking her off balance. She didn't even have time to cry out before she tumbled forward.

2

Nicolette instinctively wanted to throw her arms outward to break her descent, but that would leave Bella vulnerable. So, she did the only thing she could swiftly think to do and curled into a ball, praying nothing broke when she landed.

"Miss Nicolette!" Jane shrieked again. "Oh, you wretched, wretched animal."

Fear and horror pitched her maid's voice an octave higher.

Nicolette landed hard on her left shoulder, and a grunt escaped between her clenched teeth. *Lord,* she might've cracked a tooth. Or her shoulder. Or perhaps her hip, as well.

Bella released a terrified yelp and frantically struggled to free herself from Nicolette's vise-like grip, her little claws tearing at her spencer and gloves.

"Shh. Calm down, Bella," she soothed, struggling to retain her hold on the frightened dog. "You're all right. I'll keep you safe, darling."

Who would keep *her* safe?

By George, Nicolette hadn't suffered a humiliating fall and inevitable bruising to have that monster attack sweet Bella now. Eyes closed as she attempted to ignore the pain lancing her shoulder and side, she lashed her feet out to keep the dog away.

"Go. Away. Shoo."

Bella renewed her struggles to be free of Nicolette's arms.

"Git," Jane demanded, her voice cracking with emotion. "Git. Oh, I'm going to ring someone a peal," she promised hotly. "Where is your owner?"

"Stay, Sampson," came a melodic male voice, a great deal of concern inflecting the man's timbre.

Nicolette went perfectly still, a fresh wave of chagrin winging through her.

Really, God?

Him?

It had to be *him?*

Damnation, she groaned inwardly, for she knew that baritone voice well.

Hadn't she heard it often enough these past two years and knew full well who it belonged to? The incorrigible, dashing, perpetually cheerful and charming, Mathias Pembroke, Duke of Westfall.

As luck would have it, *he* was a good friend to *her* friends' husbands. Their graces seemed to run in a ducal pack. So wherever Sutcliffe and the other dukes were, so was Westfall. Usually with a cheeky grin on his devilishly handsome face and a seductive glint in his blue eyes.

At practically every assembly, she and her closest friends attended in Colechester and in London. Not that she'd been keeping track. After all, she wasn't interested in any particular man.

Except, if she were honest with herself, at the Christmastide house party hosted by the Duke and Duchess of Sutcliffe last December, she *had* noticed

Westfall's attentiveness to her.

What was more telling—*troubling in the extreme*—was that Nicolette hadn't rebuffed him, as she possibly should have.

Possibly?

Well, of course, she should have. At once. Immediately. Without hesitation or preamble.

Westfall was the single man to pique her interest one iota—a very, very *tiny* iota—since Kilbourne had thrown her over. And therefore, the duke was the most dangerous of men for her to associate with. Never again would she trust her instincts when it came to a man or believe a blasted thing that came from his mouth.

"Damnation, Sampson," Westfall breathed beneath his breath. "See what you've done?"

He sounded exasperated, as if he reprimanded an intractable child who'd but broken a treasured vase, rather than knocked a lady off her feet in Hyde Park.

Nicolette supposed it was too much to pray Westfall wouldn't recognize her or that he'd just collect the mongrel and go away.

Nay, he was much too much of a gentleman to do any such thing.

She refused to open her eyes just yet, however. She required a moment longer to regain her equanimity. To erect her battlements, take up her arms, and gird her loins, metaphorically speaking.

He would not rattle her composure.

She would not permit it.

Bella tried to wriggle free of her embrace, but Nicolette still feared the huge dog would make a snack of the pup.

A heartbeat later, a large, warm hand settled upon Nicolette's uninjured shoulder, and the most provocative of searing tingles radiated up her arm. And these were not painful in nature, but rather extremely arousing.

Good Lord.

"Miss Twistleton?" he inquired ever so gently in a purring voice that could melt butter. Or bones. How was she, a mere mortal, to resist such a force of nature?

I will resist.

"Can you hear me?" he asked, genuine concern

coloring his words. "Are you hurt?"

Mayhap if she pretended to have swooned…

Bella whined her frustration at still being held captive.

Yes, indeed, in a dead faint and still retaining a steely grip upon her puppy. Wholly believable.

"Well, of course, she is hurt," Jane snapped between watery sniffles, evidently her concerns for Nicolette, making her temporarily forget her place. "That lummox knocked her right off her feet, he did. Is that *thing* even a dog?" she demanded suspiciously. "He's the size of a small pony. Indeed, he might've killed her. What do you think you're doing, letting him run amuck—"

"That's quite enough, Jane," Nicolette managed in a surprisingly modulated voice. While she appreciated the girl's fervor, the maid had overstepped the mark, straight into insolence. "I assure you, both Bella and I shall survive this mishap."

One of us considerably more bruised and with a jot less dignity.

"Allow me to deliver the puppy's care into your

22

maid's capable hands so that I may assist you," Westfall cordially suggested.

Ever the gallant gentleman.

Where was his white steed?

His blindingly polished suit of armor?

Speculative whispers carried to Nicolette, and she forced her eyelids open. Her attention lit upon a wholly unwelcome threesome, and her stomach tightened as wings battered her insides.

Perfectly, bloody wonderful.

Cursing to herself, and even out loud on occasion, was another thing she now indulged in.

After all, what did it matter?

How quickly her lovely day had been spoiled, and now a dank, gray shroud of gossip fodder hovered over her.

Ladies Crustworth, Darumple, and Clutterbuck chatted fervently behind their hands, their keen attention riveted on the tableau before them. Three hell-cats whose viperish tongues could make Satan blush.

Not considered good *ton* themselves, they were

nevertheless, connected to many who were. Many who enjoyed bandying about anything that might earn them attention and disparage another in the process.

This was not good.

Not good at all.

The trio would surely embellish the incident, construing an innocent accident into a lurid clandestine meeting or something equally as preposterous.

Mama would not be pleased.

Ansley assuredly would not, either.

It was only then that Nicolette realized her lower legs, complete with her newly purchased embroidered stockings, were exposed for all to see. Another whim she'd indulged in since stepping onto the dubious path of spinsterhood.

And as luck would have it—*damn it all*—at this moment, two—no—four men unabashedly stared appreciatively at the scandalous expanse.

She couldn't conceive that they merely admired the exquisite floral stitchery.

Silent expletives and unfashionably garish stockings were one thing—well, two. But permitting gentlemen to ogle her legs? Even Nicolette could not allow that.

At once, she handed Bella to Westfall. And Bella, the traitorous little hussy, licked his face most enthusiastically, her hind end wriggling in bliss.

"Well, hello to you, too." He chuckled, that rich rumble that sent Nicolette's insides to cavorting before he passed the puppy to Jane.

Her face contorted in remorse and worry the maid crouched next to Nicolette, her serviceable gray cloak billowing around her. She clutched the pup to her chest, and Bella proceeded to exuberantly lick her chin and cheeks, drawing a giggle from Jane.

"Bella, stop," she said between laughs, angling her round face away.

His big brown eyes hopeful, Sampson thumped his rope-like tail thrice but didn't move. He shifted his soulful eyes to Westfall, fairly pleading for permission to greet Bella.

"Good boy," Westfall praised. "Stay there."

The duke's beautiful mouth tipped into a chagrined smile as he cut Jane a sideways glance, a hint of mirth twinkling in his indigo blue eyes. "He won't hurt the puppy, I promise you. He just wants to say hello. He's actually quite gentle."

Yes, Nicolette had experienced his *gentleness,* first-hand.

Jane slowly straightened, clutching Bella to her as if she feared Sampson would gobble her for a morning snack.

"So you say, but that—" She cast her disparaging gaze over him as if trying to summon an accurate description—"That *oaf* just knocked Miss Nicolette down."

"He's still a puppy and forgets his manners. He also has no concept of how large he is," Westfall apologized.

He looked far too striking in his dark blue jacket for Nicolette's peace of mind. The color accented his eyes to perfection and gave his jet-black hair beneath his chimney-style top hat a bluish tint.

She bit the inside of her cheek, all the while mentally chiding herself for noticing.

"Hmph." Jane made a disbelieving noise and

pinched her lips together.

"He escaped the footman walking him," the duke said by way of an explanation.

Obviously.

Look away, Nicolette commanded herself.

She did so with a degree of disinclination that didn't portend well. Focusing her attention on Sampson, she asked, "Is he yours? I thought your mother only kept Pomeranians as pets."

She almost laughed at the absurdity of the question.

Here she lay indelicately on the pathway, several *haut ton* members gawping at her, and she casually chatted about his mother's notoriously spoiled Pomeranians.

"I'm minding him for a friend," Westfall elucidated, patting the dog's oversized head.

In truth, he looked more bear-like than canine. "What breed is he?"

"He's a Newfoundland. They were bred to be work and rescue dogs."

"Are they all so large?" she asked.

Westfall lifted a shoulder. "More or less."

Sampson stared longingly at Bella, who eyed him with cautious interest.

"Are you injured, Miss Twistleton?" Westfall inquired solicitously again. "Do you require a physician?"

Do I?

No, nothing felt broken.

However, Nicolette's shoulder and ankle ached like the very devil, her hip not quite as much.

"That will not be necessary," she said, shaking her head.

Ouch.

She winced slightly, sorer than she'd at first realized. She didn't relish the walk home on her tender ankle or the speculation her soiled gown was bound to produce, however. Mama might forbid her to walk out alone, henceforth.

"Hmm." Westfall made a low sound in his throat, but Nicolette couldn't discern its meaning. For as long as she'd known him, he'd done that.

The crowd continued to increase around them, and

she still lay splayed indecorously on the footpath. Before she had a chance to adjust her pale pink walking gown, Westfall gently hauled her into a sitting position.

"Your gown," he murmured beneath his breath, his gaze politely averted from her legs.

Her face burning, she shoved her skirts down. As she did so, her bonnet slid off, and several strands of dark hair tumbled loose over her shoulders and breast.

He made an inarticulate sound, and she speared him a questioning glance.

He was so close, she could see the midnight blue ring encircling his irises, and the gold flecks there, too. She would not—*no, you will not*—peek a glance at the granite thighs covered in cream-colored pantaloons, so close to her, she could see the outline of his corded thigh muscles.

What the hell was wrong with her?

Noticing a man's thighs?

Nicolette's stomach pitched in the weirdest fashion.

Perhaps she *was* hurt worse than she'd first

thought.

Had she hit her head, as well?

She cautiously moved her neck slightly to test the theory.

The movement didn't meet with so much as a single twinge.

Westfall perused the onlookers encircling them and motioned for a tall, blond man in green and gold livery to come forward. "Farrow, please collect Sampson and take him home."

"Yes, sir." At once, the footman sprang forward and seized the brown leather leash that, until now, Nicolette hadn't even noticed.

But then again, when she'd seen Sampson lumbering toward her, she'd feared Bella or she were about to be attacked and mauled.

As Farrow led the docile behemoth away, Westfall's censorious attention roved the gawkers again. A degree of marble hardened his amiable features and leeched into his voice as well. "The rest of you may go on your way. As you can see, Miss Twistleton is fine. Thank you for your concern."

Oh, well done, Your Grace.

Nicolette only just managed to check her grin of approval. She held no great admiration for the threesome, unlike the elevated opinions they had of themselves.

Lady Clutterbuck opened her mouth as if to object.

However, Lady Darumple clutched her friend's boney elbow, fiercely whispered something in her ear, and steered her friend away. Her eyes tightening disapprovingly at the corners, with a last considering glance, Lady Crustworth elevated her nose and swept away, too.

Absently rubbing her throbbing ankle, Nicolette strove to conceive of a delicate way to rise that didn't include rolling onto all fours and presenting her bum for viewing.

Without so much as a by your leave or a hint of what he was about to do, Westfall slipped an arm beneath her knees and the other around her shoulders and lifted her. His muscles flexed and bunched with the effort, but no hint of strain marred his face.

Her breath lodged in her throat, and she struggled to formulate a single word.

"My curricle is just there." He jutted his strong, square chin in the direction of the entrance. "I shall see you home."

Nicolette stiffened, prepared to give him a proper set down.

Of all the high-handed—

"Should I come with you, Miss Nicolette?" Jane, her eyes round as the moon, shifted her astonished gaze between them several times.

He grinned, a distinctly devilish glint in his blue eyes. "I'm afraid the conveyance only seats two, Miss...?"

"Pirdie, Your Grace. Jane Pirdie." She bobbed a wobbly curtsy.

Nicolette snorted and almost rolled her eyes.

Now she decides to remember her manners?

Westfall sliced Nicolette a wicked grin. He'd heard her snort.

"Miss Pirdie, hurry home and make them aware there's been an accident. Send someone for the physician, too," Westfall suggested, adjusting his hold on Nicolette, and angling her higher in his arms.

Her heart *did not* turn over from excitement or from a rush of sensation. It was a fear of being dumped unceremoniously onto the ground that caused the irregular fluttering and flitting about behind her ribcage.

"Yes, Your Grace." Still holding a whimpering Bella, Jane turned on her heel and rushed away, her cloak flapping about her ankles.

Flabbergasted, Nicolette stared after her.

Why, she's abandoned me.

"Your Grace," Nicolette objected, flames licking at her face and all too aware the onlookers had yet to disburse completely. "Do put me down at once," she hissed into his ear, clutching at his entirely too broad and muscular shoulders for fear of taking another tumble.

Westfall, was after all, well over six feet tall.

She might've also have caught a delicious whiff of his manly scent. And she did not lower her nose a fraction to inhale his cologne. She'd simply adjusted the angle of her neck.

Liar.

"Shh, relax." His rich voice held a playful note. He gave her thighs a little squeeze, and a pulse of desire trilled through her.

Relax? Was he utterly mad?

"This is most inappropriate," she said under her breath, forcing calm and modulation to her tone. She couldn't very well screech like a harpy even if it would be ever so satisfying. "Whatever will people think, Your Grace?"

Another few strands of hair escaped her pins, and he grinned as they cascaded down her back.

This assuredly wasn't the type of adventure she'd wished for no more than ten minutes ago.

"I can hardly permit you to hobble home on your injured ankle, Miss Twistleton."

He glanced down, and once again, she was taken by the shade of his blue eyes and the annoyingly perfect lines of his well-defined face. It was much easier to resist a man if he had bad breath, body odor, or a razor rash.

"I am inadvertently responsible for your injuries," he continued. "And therefore, it is my duty to ensure you arrive at your residence and are examined by a physician."

Everything he's said was practical and, in truth, correct.

"But—" she started to protest.

He flashed that sinful grin again, and she swore he was enjoying himself.

"Besides, your maid just left you in my care." His voice took on a rather thrilling and oh-so-naughty timbre, and she trembled.

"It wouldn't do at all for you to be seen walking without a chaperone, my dear. Think of your *reputation*." Sarcasm fairly dripped from his conciliatory tone, and he had the ballocks—*the absolute ballocks!*—to waggle his eyebrows.

Nicolette wanted to hit him.

She really and truly did. And she wasn't given to violence or aggression.

She couldn't help think he took liberties because of their mutual friends and their long acquaintance.

That didn't sit well, and Lord knew the *ton* would be in a dither over the day's events.

Why he, of all men, should stir such a primal response baffled her to no end. Instead, she pinched his neck, though, with her gloves on, it scarcely counted as a *real* pinch.

"Ow! You little hellion." He shot her a surprised look, a spark of something undefinable but, nevertheless, tantalizing shining in his eyes. "Out for your pound of flesh, eh?"

"*You*, Westfall, are compromising my reputation," she said through clenched teeth as she peeked over his shoulder, positive she'd see people staring after them.

She was right.

"Oh, Lord." Closing her eyes, she groaned. "They're still watching us, Mathias."

"*Mathias*?" he murmured suggestively, his eyes smoldering. "May *I* presume to call you Nicolette?"

Good God.

"You may not." Between his voice and eyes, she'd be a pile of smoldering cinders if she permitted any such thing.

This situation grew worse with every passing second.

"Do you know your eyes fairly flash blue fire, when you are peeved?" he asked, conversationally.

She chose to ignore his question.

"I cannot imagine what tales they will spread. This could very well see us both ruined, Your Grace."

"Nonsense. I'm merely assisting a damsel in distress," he said airily, striding along as if she weighed no more than Bella. "How can they find fault with that?"

Oh, they'd find fault, even if they had to contrive twaddle themselves.

"*You* are no knight in shining armor," she muttered, peevishly.

Chivalry and gallantry had gone by the wayside centuries ago. Men nowadays—except for Ansley and a select few others—only cared about one thing. *Themselves.*

No, that wasn't accurate.

They cared about five things: themselves, drink, gambling, bit o' muslins, and horses.

The Duke of Westfall glanced down, a challenging grin slanting across his strong, tempting mouth. "I've never taken you for the melodramatic sort, Miss Twistleton."

"You, sir, well know how rumors start," she snapped, far too aware of the sinewy arms holding her and the very masculine wall of his chest pressing into her injured side. Heat exuded from him, and it was all she could do not to snuggle closer and hold him tightly. Dangerous musings, indeed, for an avowed spinster.

"I don't even want to think of what will be said about us," she said, cringing at her strident tenor.

Was she well on her way to becoming a crotchety old tabby already?

Mayhap she should acquire a dozen cats and a few moth-eaten shawls, too. And a cane. A scandalous one with a shockingly engraved handle. And she'd only wear one color—scarlet—ever.

Whether the increasingly painful throb in her shoulder and ankle or the genuine fear their names would be on every gossipmonger's tongue before day's end caused her heightened temper, she couldn't guess.

Indeed, it had nothing to do with the peculiar flutters and sensations assailing her.

Did the duke have to smell so bloody divine, too?

Peppermint and starch and sandalwood and perhaps a hint of brandy or whisky?

A hundred winged insects of some sort took flight in her belly. The feeling was rather heady and unlike anything she'd ever experienced before.

"Rest assured, Miss Twistleton, I shall quell any gossip." He winked and flashed that devil-may-care smile again. "We dukes can do that."

Nicolette's mind went blank as a sheet of foolscap for a blink, and then a horrendous, ghastly, catastrophic epiphany struck with the force of a sailing schooner's foremast cudgeling her.

And, *good Lord,* if she didn't find herself gaping in utter disbelief, unable to accept the insight.

Her ragged breath stalled for several heartbeats.

No, she instantly denied.

She'd been so diligent. So cautious. So, so punctilious.

It wasn't possible.

Yes. It is.

She, Nicolette Adelia Estelle Twistleton, a woman sworn to never succumb to a man's charms again, was attracted to Mathias. And while not precisely a *roué* nor a rakehell, neither was he a pillar of morality and respectability.

Her bruised heart could not stand to be shattered again. Most especially by the captivatingly charming and irresistibly handsome Duke of Westfall.

God, curse her for a nincompoop.

Booby. Numpty. Peagoose.

She was not—*by all that is holy, I am not*—making that mistake again. To do so would be the height of folly.

Only, Nicolette feared it was already too late.

3

Grosvenor Square, Mayfair

Afternoon

16 May 1810

Mathias smiled at the footman as he passed Romulus's reins to him. "I shan't be above thirty minutes."

Likely, far less.

It would only take a few moments to ascertain if Nicolette was well on her way to recovery and apologize again for Sampson's poor manners.

Tipping his hat at a pair of curious, haughty ladies as they passed by, and then catching a glimpse of a familiar face practically pressed against the carriage glass as the conveyance rolled past, he reconsidered the wisdom of this decision.

If he wasn't mistaken, the beady-eyed, pinched-faced meddler peering at him from behind the conveyance's window had been none other than Lady Gloria Darumple—rumormonger, extraordinaire. Many a *le beau monde* member had been scarred by that woman's rancorous tongue.

Damn his eyes.

His presence outside the Twistletons' house today, combined with the event in Hyde Park yesterday, would have the chinwag conjuring all manner of inaccurate assumptions. If he wasn't mindful, he'd see an announcement in the gossip rags connecting his name with Nicolette's.

He'd not have called on her at all today, except he felt responsible for her injuries. Sampson had been left in his care, after all, and would remain so until his owner, Landry Audsley, Earl of Keyworth, returned from the continent next month.

Odd that Keyworth hadn't left the pup at his

country seat.

Rolling a shoulder, Mathias dismissed the thought. Keyworth frequently did unexpected things.

It had been pure luck that Mathias had driven by Hyde Park yesterday on his way to White's. He'd spied Sampson racing pell-mell across the greens as a very flustered Farrow sprinted after him, his coattails flapping furiously in his wake.

Now, two footmen were assigned to take Sampson on his outings.

As Mathias crossed the pavement to the house, a blue tit alit on the branch of a purple lilac bush.

Manicured gardens, boasting a profusion of flowers, including peonies, irises, and lily of the valley, flanked a well-scrubbed stairway with scrolled wrought-iron handrails leading to the house. The subtle, heady scent surrounding Nicolette yesterday as he carried her through Hyde Park had hinted of peonies, lily of the valley, and lilac.

Perhaps she created her own perfume.

The blue sky, with only a few wispy clouds feathered across the horizon, heralded another mild spring day, and he regretted that Nicolette's ankle confined her to the indoors. Perhaps the Twistletons' had a back patio or terrace from which she might enjoy the unseasonably pleasant afternoon.

Mayhap he could persuade her to take a turn in Hyde Park or ride Rotten Row with him soon. In full bloom, the cherry blossoms gave the pathways a fairylike quality, especially when the petals fluttered from the trees during a breeze, swirling to the ground like pink snow.

As Mathias climbed the stairs, he glanced up at the tidy, brick house. Not as large and ostentatious as many of the manors in the square, it was, nonetheless, quite charming. If he recalled correctly, Scarborough had come into the title after an uncle had died. Until then, the Twistletons had spent most of their time in the country.

Scarborough.

Now there was an interesting fellow—reserved, methodical, severe. Some even called him unfriendly and standoffish. Mathias had perceived Scarborough's aloofness to stem from the discomfort of being in the public eye and from having an earldom unexpectedly thrust upon him.

How very different Ansley Twistleton, Earl of Scarborough, was from his vivacious sister.

Their coloring was similar, both possessing raven-black hair and vivid blue eyes. But as far as Mathias had observed, that was where the resemblances ended. Scarborough generally lingered on the periphery of social functions, watching—if he attended at all. Nicolette, on the other hand, was always in the middle of whatever excitement was occurring.

Not that Nicolette Twistleton couldn't—and didn't—regularly take a man down a peg or two. She'd perfected her wintery blue-eyed stare to an art, and cutting ripostes and witticisms easily rolled off her tongue. Wearing a winsome smile, she verbally filleted any dandy or swain who overstepped.

Mathias, thus far, had been spared her displeasure, despite the numerous occasions they'd been in mixed company together. Well, except for yesterday when the vixen had pinched him. And that merely proved that she wasn't impervious to him.

A pleased grin tilted his mouth as he briskly rapped upon the ruby-colored door.

The flush pinkening her ivory cheeks and the plump pillows of her pretty mouth pursed in annoyance couldn't hide the spark of interest in her stunning gaze. Her big, almond-shaped eyes were, in a word, exquisite.

Indeed, the most mesmerizing eyes Mathias had ever seen.

He quite lost himself when he looked into them. Which belied explanation, as he'd gazed into many beautiful women's eyes and enjoyed the feminine charms of several willing women, as well.

Framed by a fringe of lush ebony lashes beneath winged brows, Nicolette's eyes were a shade somewhere between forget-me-nots and periwinkle. And always a hint of distrust, betrayal, and pain shadowed their enigmatic depths, although she veiled her emotions well.

Nevertheless, they were noticeable if one was discerning and took the time to probe beyond the various barriers she'd erected.

It pleased him no end to discover Nicolette wasn't as resistant to masculine regard as she affected. Well, *his* regard, that was. Mathias certainly hoped to God it was only *his* attention that rattled her composure. He'd been biding his time for so long, patiently waiting for her to notice him as her heart and spirit healed.

The alternative made his blood sing with something somewhat dark and unpleasant. Something foreign and possessive and alarming in its intensity. Why Nicolette should be the sole woman to ignite whatever this thing was, he didn't ponder. He only knew the more time he spent with her, the more he wanted to be with the winsome woman.

Much like a tippler and his gin.

She could easily become an addiction, and then what was he to do?

She had felt something as he carried her, too, though he'd wager she'd bite off her tongue before admitting to any such thing.

Mathias knew, of course, of her broken betrothal. Also knew her reputation for flirting and teasing and then eviscerating any man stupid enough to show more than a passing interest in her. Hence, he'd studiously stayed on the perimeter, safe and unthreatening.

Nicolette enticed men into her web, and then when they were caught, much like a spider's attack, she stabbed them with her rapier-sharp tongue.

She was a contradictory, fascinating, and wholly beguiling mélange.

Rather than put him off, it intrigued the hell out of him.

It helped that he understood and even empathized with her jaded attitude and behavior.

Prior to inheriting the dukedom four years ago, he'd also experienced a broken betrothal. By a woman who wasn't satisfied with becoming the lowly Mrs. Mathias Pembroke, even if his purse had jingled quite nicely back then.

Thanks to several lucrative investments, including acquiring three ships, said purse clinked much, *much* more so now.

Victoria had coveted a title before her name, and had flung him off with the same disregard one did the contents of a tosspot when the middling-aged Viscount

Calbraith had come sniffing around the young beauty.

Mathias had been her back-up plan; in case she couldn't catch a bigger fish her first Season—a peer to be precise. And he'd been ignorant of her machinations until he'd caught her in an *indelicate* situation with Calbraith at a house party.

Soon after she'd married the viscount, Mathias came to appreciate he'd escaped a dreadful life sentence. His infatuation with Victoria gradually faded into disdain and, to a degree, pity for her husband, who had seemed to genuinely care for the fickle chit.

She was rumored to have had one affair after another since becoming a viscountess. Apparently, her aging husband couldn't satisfy her *needs*.

Fate most definitely had a wickedly perverse sense of humor.

For now, Mathias was the well-respected and popular Duke of Westfall, and Viscountess Victoria Calbraith was a widow living on society's fringes. If chitchat was accurate, her pockets were to let, as well, and she urgently sought a wealthy husband to remedy that condition.

Evidently, once she'd settled her quest for a title, she'd decided money was rather a necessity, after all. Calbraith might've had a respected centuries' old title, but he'd been living on credit for years and was reputed to have been a pinch-penny.

Recently, Victoria had approached Mathias at a rout and had shamelessly offered to renew their relationship. "*We can take right up where we left off, Mathias, darling,*" she suggested while skimming her hand across his groin with a practiced touch. He sincerely doubted she'd come by her expertise with her doddering, decrepitude of a husband.

Even now, Mathias's mouth filled with distaste at the notion of bedding her.

Not, by God, if bloody hell freezes over.

In point of fact, she offered herself to him right there, had even proposed they find a library or another vacant room for an intimate dalliance. She'd very explicitly suggested one similar to that which he'd stumbled upon involving her and Calbraith. It seemed she had a penchant for being taken over the back of sofas, divans, settees…

He'd succinctly declined her offer, turned on his heel and left Victoria standing alone, a piqued pout upon her mouth, and vexation sparkling in her eyes.

Even more ironic was the truth surrounding Mathias's birth. A dirty little family secret—the proverbial skeleton in the closet.

Another grin pulled his mouth up on one side.

There was a strong probability that he shouldn't hold the ducal title at all.

However, no one besides his mother knew the truth behind that most carefully guarded secret. And as exposure would destroy his mother and sister, Mathias would take that ugliness to his grave. He'd not even tell his wife when the day came that he wed, lest such a secret might slip out.

It was good his mother couldn't identify the hell's spawn who'd violated her three decades ago, else Mathias would've done everything within his power to ruin the fiend. For all of his genial outward appearance, he possessed a dark temper. Though seldom stirred, when aroused, his wrath was an ominous, unforgiving entity that demanded revenge.

His father and mother had been in love and planning to wed. Upon learning what had happened to his beloved, Matthew Pembroke promptly married her. Mathias had been born eight-and one-half months later, and Father had claimed him as his own without hesitation.

Neither his mother or father knew for sure whether Matthew or the rapist was Mathias's sire. To his credit, Matthew Pembroke had raised Mathias as if he were his progeny because Father had loved unconditionally.

The world had lost an exceptionally good and decent man when he'd died a decade ago.

Assuredly, as a distant cousin to the previous duke, Father had never conceived Mathias would inherit the duchy. Mathias wasn't about to terminate his ventures in spice, coffee, tea, silk, and cotton trade merely because he'd inherited an unwanted title.

So, what if he smelled of the shop?

He enjoyed working, and he was proud of his accomplishments and of the people his enterprises employed. Far better to dirty his hands with honest work than to lounge about all day, a useless coxcomb.

Mathias foresaw a future where the peerage no longer wielded power and control as it did today, and if *le beau monde* didn't adapt, many noble families could conceivably find themselves impoverished.

As he raised his hand to knock again, the door ever-so-slowly swung open.

Before him stood an austere, entirely bald butler possessing the most remarkable pair of eyebrows Mathias had ever observed. The pillow-like pouches beneath the majordomo's jaundiced gaze valiantly competed for attention. Nonetheless, the grizzled brows, which appeared very much like wrestling gray caterpillars, won the contest, hands down.

"May I be of assistance?" the butler asked in a dirge-like tone.

Generally, when one knocks upon a door, that is the case.

Mathias checked his glib response.

"Indeed, you may." Deciding agreeableness would get him further, he procured a crisp calling card with gold and royal blue script and extended it toward the ram-rod stiff butler. "The Duke of Westfall to see Miss

Twistleton."

Those impressive eyebrows rose a quarter-inch and jousted with one another.

Mathias tried not to stare, but honestly, they were the most extraordinary things. It was as if each row of wiry hair possessed a life of its own.

"Is Miss Twistleton expecting you?" How did he manage to speak without an iota of inflection in his voice?

The servant quite obviously wasn't impressed by Mathias's title, nor did he believe Nicolette awaited his visit.

"No—"

"Reeves?" a woman inquired, her tone curious rather than critical. "Who is at the door?"

A distinctly aggrieved expression flitted across Reeves's face as he turned toward the entry while intentionally blocking the doorway with his body.

What? Did he think Mathias would force his way inside?

"His Grace, the Duke of Westfall, Mrs. Twistleton."

"Well, do not leave the man standing on the stoop, for heaven's sake. Whatever can you be thinking?" she said, her voice growing more distinct as she moved closer. "His grace did us a tremendous service yesterday, Reeves, seeing our darling Nicolette home after she'd been injured in the park."

"Indeed," Reeves droned, stepping aside and permitting Mathias entrance with the enthusiasm of a man allowing a convicted serial killer into his bedchamber. "Your Grace."

It occurred to Mathias the old gent only protected his young mistress, and respect for the servant encompassed him. He produced his most appreciative smile.

"Thank you, Reeves. Your diligence is commendable."

Reeves's brows settled into their usual place upon his noble forehead, and a degree of frostiness dissipated, increasing his welcome from frigid arctic to icy condescension. His features once more a banal mask of indifference, he inclined his head and accepted Mathias's hat.

"Your Grace." Mrs. Twistleton, a handsome woman, greatly resembling her daughter, except her eyes were brown instead of flower blue and time had etched fine lines across her forehead, the corner of her eyes, and around her mouth, glided forth, her hands outstretched. "What a delightful surprise. With all of the commotion yesterday, I didn't have an opportunity to properly thank you for assisting Nicolette."

"I was glad to be of service." Mathias bowed over her hand. As he straightened, he said, "Please forgive me for calling unannounced, but I feel responsible for her condition. It was a dog in my care that caused the incident."

A duke could call at any hour, day or night, and no host would openly object. He, however, didn't abuse his privilege and power as many in his position were wont to do.

Yesterday, he'd managed to briefly explain how Nicolette had acquired her injuries, but Mrs. Twistleton had been understandably distracted. With a hurried thanks, she'd directed the footmen to carry her protesting daughter to her bedchamber. Face pale and pleated with concern, Mrs. Twistleton had ascended directly behind them without bidding him farewell.

And all the while, Nicolette had doggedly maintained she was *perfectly fine*, and carrying her was *entirely unnecessary*.

He appreciated her independent streak and her mulishness, too. In truth, there wasn't much about the wholly delectable, exasperatingly captivating Nicolette Twistleton he didn't enjoy.

A grin playing around the edges of his mouth, Mathias had waited until he no longer heard her objecting before taking his leave.

"How fares she today?" he asked, taking in the bouquet of pink and fuchsia peonies on a marble-topped mahogany half-table below an ornate gold mirror. "Improving, I hope?"

An intricately patterned parquet floor graced the entrance along with a sea green velvet-covered bench and two chairs with matching upholstered seats.

Everything about the entry bespoke comfort and good taste, and understated elegance, rather than an intent to impress. Well, the Twistletons had been landed gentry before Scarborough inherited, and it seemed they'd implemented their country preferences in London.

Admirable of them. They hadn't let the *ton's* dictates sway them.

Another glimpse of the flowers caused him to tighten his mouth.

Should he have brought posies for Nicolette as a token to wish her a speedy recovery?

No, already tongues wagged out of control. Arriving on the Twistletons' doorstep, flowers in hand, would have them wed in a fortnight by special license.

"My daughter doesn't take well to being indisposed, Your Grace." A half-smile tipping her mouth upward, Mrs. Twistleton cut him a somewhat sardonic glance. "In point of fact, she refused to stay abed today as Dr. Simmons ordered, and is even now, sitting on the patio, reading."

Nicolette's obstinance didn't surprise Mathias, and that she was up and about relieved him immensely. Her injuries must've been as mild as she'd insisted they were, else she'd not have been able to descend the stairs.

"I am relieved to hear she is mending well." That ride in the park might take place sooner than he'd anticipated, and giddy anticipation sparked through him.

Another smile wreathing her face, Mrs. Twistleton guided him down the corridor, and through a pleasant green-themed salon featuring several potted plants and airy landscape paintings. It was as if this room was meant to replicate the countryside the family so favored.

"Please do say you'll stay for tea, Your Grace. I'm sure Nicolette would be glad of the company." Genuine concern for her daughter seemed to motivate her, rather than any calculations or match-making schemes.

A most refreshing change, Mathias must admit.

"Before you arrived, I asked Reeves to serve us on the terrace," Mrs. Twistleton explained. "Such a pleasant day shouldn't be wasted indoors."

"Indeed," he murmured politely.

She looked over her shoulder.

"At Fawtonbrooke Hall, we frequently take tea and picnics on the greens. There's a lovely folly with a charming view of a pond. It's one of Nicolette's favorite places. She says the folly reminds her of Grecian architecture." She chuckled and shook her head. "My daughter does so long to travel to other parts of the world, but her brother and I have no such penchant, much to her dismay."

Poor Nicolette.

She was a caged bird, flitting against a gilded prison and longing to take to wing. Whoever was lucky enough to set her free, would no doubt see her soar. Pondering his poetic musings, he swung the door open, and Mrs. Twistleton preceded him through.

Suddenly finding himself eager to prolong his visit, Mathias mentally calculated the rest of his afternoon. His sister, Megan, and their mother weren't expecting him until half-past four.

Yes, he could spare an hour for tea. Particularly if it meant time with Nicolette.

"I'd be delighted to stay," he heard himself saying, practically before he'd finished his thought.

Careful, old chap. Don't get ahead of yourself.

"Excellent," Mrs. Twistleton said, a genuine smile bending her mouth as they stepped onto the pavers.

One of the things he appreciated about all of the Twistletons was their lack of artifice.

"Cook made lemon Shrewsbury biscuits." Leaning in conspiratorially, she lowered her voice. "They're Nicolette's favorite. She adores anything with lemon. She didn't eat her dinner or breakfast, and barely touched her midday meal, so I do hope the biscuits will tempt her. She's already lost so much weight."

Worry etched her features as they settled on her daughter, and the line of her mouth thinned.

Understanding dawned, and Mathias comprehended how difficult it must be for Mrs. Twistleton to protect her daughter from further hurt and yet encourage Nicolette to face her fears. To allow herself a different future than the course she was presently set upon.

Spinsterhood.

Of its own volition, his gaze sought her.

She sat with her legs resting on a dark burgundy

61

chaise lounge, no doubt brought outside for her comfort. Her puppy lay on her lap, and as she read, she idly petted the sleeping dog.

Nicolette looked content and more peaceful than he'd seen her in a long while. Her serenity enhanced her beauty, and Mathias found himself staring, entranced.

"Darling," Mrs. Twistleton said, a shade too brightly. "Look who has joined us for tea."

4

Mrs. Twistleton's exuberant declaration yanked Mathias back to the present.

She bustled forward, motioning to Reeves approaching with measured steps from the other direction with a laden tray.

Nicolette glanced upward. Her beautiful eyes rounded, and her equally pretty mouth slackened in astonishment upon spying Mathias. At once, she snapped her mouth and novel closed simultaneously. She swiftly tucked the book beside her, very deliberately pulling the fabric of her white muslin gown atop it.

Hiding it, is she?

Just what had the ever-so-unapproachable Nicolette Twistleton been reading?

From the becoming color skating up the gentle slope of her cheeks, he'd wager it hadn't been prose by Mrs. Wollstonecraft, Olympe de Gouges, or Voltaire.

Interesting.

Her mother didn't seem to have noticed or else was aware of her daughter's choice of reading material and had no objection.

"Thank you, Reeves," Mrs. Twistleton said as she set about organizing the contents of the tray.

"Madam." Reeves dipped his head and departed, one precise footstep after another.

Mathias bowed before Nicolette, admiring her shiny raven hair, pulled into a simple chignon, and the pearl earbobs dangling from her shell-like ears. Her empire style gown with a lavender ribbon below her bosoms emphasized her creamy décolletage, though the neckline could hardly be considered risqué.

She was a fresh spring flower. A beautiful blossom on the verge of blooming.

God's ballocks.

Since when did *he* wax poetic?

In truth, more and more so secretly for some time now. Ever since, a certain young woman became eligible on the Marriage Mart once more.

"Miss Twistleton. I trust you are recovering from your mishap yesterday?" Mathias asked, careful to keep his tone polite, but impartial lest she erect her defenses.

"Mama would have me rest in bed for several days." Nicolette elevated a wry eyebrow as she cut her mother busily attending the tea tray a side-eyed glance. "But, in truth, other than a few bruises, I'm fine. My ankle scarcely hurts at all. It's not even swollen. See."

As if to emphasize her point, she pulled her gown up a fraction and wiggled said ankle, which today was covered in another pair of colorfully embroidered stockings. Delicate pink and purple flowers clung to a green vine that climbed from a trim ankle to disappear under her gown's ruffled hem.

Why, for all of her outward appearance of banal propriety, Miss Nicolette Twistleton had a secretive, bold streak. Were any of her other small-clothes similarly embellished?

The intimate thought caused an instant pulse to his groin.

Despite his earlier intentions, Mathias grinned wickedly and gave her a bold wink, very much appreciating the well-turned ankle. "You look *very well*, indeed."

"*Men.*" Rolling her eyes, she snorted and shoved her gown back down and muttered, 'It's just an ankle, for pity's sake."

Aye, connected to a very graceful calf, connected to a supple thigh, connected to—

"Your Grace?" Mrs. Twistleton indicated a nearby rattan chair.

What?

He blinked blankly, a very erotic image of her daughter lodged in his imagination and obscuring all else.

What had she said?

Oh, yes. Tea.

Mathias shook off his sensual musings, determinedly ignoring the distinct throb in his nether regions. Hell, he'd better get a grip on his lust or he'd be sporting a cockstand. Somewhat tricky to explain *that* away during tea. To his knowledge, neither tea nor biscuits roused a man's lust to the point of chagrin.

He sank into the indicated chair with relief. At least when he sat, his partial erection wasn't as noticeable.

His hostess had already claimed his chair's mate and held a delicate, scalloped edged teacup in her hand. "Milk or sugar?"

"Neither, thank you." After examining the assortment of dainties, he helped himself to a ginger biscuit, using the opportunity to rearrange his coat slightly.

Better.

"Ah, just so for Nicolette, as well," she all but crooned.

Taking a bite, he considered Mrs. Twistleton.

Hmm, perhaps he'd misread her after all, for her gaze now bore a distinctly shrewd glint as she looked between him and her daughter. Until this moment, he hadn't taken Mary Twistleton to be a matchmaker.

"Did you truly call merely to check on my progress?" Nicolette eyed him suspiciously, those marvelous blue eyes of her slightly tense at the corners. "I confess, that seems highly out of character for *you*."

Her unwarranted barb stung until Mathias reminded himself, she used her sharp tongue as a weapon to protect herself.

Or to scrape barnacles off ships, bark from trees, paint from wood.

It seemed in his case, she'd decided to go on the offense and rebuff him.

Which begged the question, why did she feel the need?

Because of the attraction, she'd valiantly tried to hide yesterday?

He hid his delighted grin behind his cup of fragrant oolong tea. Quite possibly, the tea he'd imported.

Nicolette would be highly vexed if she knew he was onto her ploy.

Mathias had shaken her carefully constructed

walls in Hyde Park. That momentary weakness had allowed him a glimpse of the woman she kept judiciously concealed behind a barricade of cynicism. The woman who'd captivated his interest quite some time ago.

Over two years ago, to be exact.

A woman he never conceived that he would have the opportunity to court. First, because she'd been betrothed. Secondly, because she now affected to despise all men.

"Nicolette," her mother admonished, taken aback. "Where are your manners, my dear?"

She softened her chastisement with a doting smile as she handed her daughter her steaming tea along with a lemon Shrewsbury biscuit.

Upon spying the treat, Nicolette's eyes lit, and a delighted smile blossomed over her face. "Oh," she breathed. "Cook baked my favorites."

Her frank joy at something so trivial hitched Mathias's breath in his lungs. He'd never seen her so unguarded, and the woman before him radiating such happiness transfixed him.

Careful, old chap, he sternly warned himself for the second time in the past few minutes. *Don't wade in over your head. You very well might drown.*

Hell, he was far past that point. Had been for a good while.

In truth, he suspected she'd laid claim to his heart during the Christmastide festivities at the Sutcliffes' house party.

He finished chewing the supremely delicious ginger biscuit before responding. Their cook was truly gifted. "In truth, I hoped I might persuade you and your mother to accompany me to the theater the day after tomorrow."

Where the hell had *that* come from?

It wasn't a premeditated plan, but it was the perfect solution to the slight dilemma he had.

He glanced at Nicolette's ankle, now regretfully covered by her gown. "If you're well enough, that is."

Her puppy stirred, opening sleepy eyes and yawning. She stood, and after stretching, climbed up her mistress's torso, demanding a bite of biscuit.

"No, Bella, you cannot have mine." Nicolette set

the pug on the ground and then broke a piece off another biscuit for the puppy.

"What a generous offer, Your Grace." Mrs. Twistleton couldn't quite keep the giddiness from her voice, but to her credit, she hadn't accepted on her daughter's behalf. That didn't prevent her from giving her daughter a half-pleading, half-expectant look.

"I assure you, Your Grace, you needn't go to such extremes as recompense for Sampson tackling me to the ground." A hint of mischief gleamed in Nicolette's eyes, and her pretty mouth twitched the merest bit. "You've apologized, and I've accepted. Let us be done with the matter, shall we?"

A crestfallen expression replaced her mother's earlier exuberance.

Bella trotted over to sniff him. She placed her front paws upon his calf, begging for a treat with her buggy little eyes. He broke off a bit of biscuit, and after glancing at Nicolette for permission, he gave the puppy the snack.

"She's hopelessly spoiled, already," Nicolette said fondly.

Bella dropped onto her haunches and chewed happily.

"You would be doing me the greatest favor," he insisted, wiping his fingers on his serviette. "My sister has recently returned to England after living abroad these past eight years. Her husband was a diplomat stationed in India." He picked up his cup, aware of the reflective look Nicolette leveled him. "In truth, she's just come out of mourning and has few acquaintances in London."

"The poor dear," Mrs. Twistleton murmured. "My sincere condolences."

"Indeed," Nicolette echoed. "How hard to suffer such a tragic loss so far from home and family."

"True." He helped himself to a Shrewsbury biscuit. They *were* particularly delicious. "Though she's a strong woman and has three sons to help ease her grief."

"Ah, yes. I certainly understand that." Mrs. Twistleton gave Nicolette a fond smile. "I do not know what I would've done without my children when my dear husband passed. They gave me a purpose, a reason to rise every morn."

Nicolette returned her mother's adoring smile before taking a dainty bite of biscuit. A crumb lingered on her lower lip, and she darted her tongue out to catch the tidbit.

Mathias swallowed, his mind at once jumping to all of the other things she might do with her tongue.

God rot him for a lecher.

"Megan left England directly after marrying," Mathias put in, dragging his mind away from things he had no business woolgathering about. "I hope to introduce her around and help take her mind off Michael's unexpected passing."

Nicolette's expression softened, and she curved her mouth into a sympathetic smile.

He barely restrained his victorious grin.

"In that case, I should like to attend the theater to meet your sister."

Sly vixen.

Nicolette made it clear she only agreed to attend to assist with his sister.

So be it.

It was a first step in extracting her from the prickly shell Nicolette had surrounded herself with. Why he'd appointed himself to take on the task, he had no idea. Except he would see her happyand the haunted look that lingered in the depths of her eyes for so long, banished for good.

Again, he didn't carefully examine why he so desired to see her happy once more.

"As would I," Mrs. Twistleton remarked, reminding Mathias of her presence.

"What are you reading, Miss Twistleton?" He asked innocently, his gaze gravitating to the rectangular lump beneath her skirt.

It was wicked of him to tease her.

Her gaze shot to his, and a tell-tale color bloomed across her cheeks. "Ah... A book—"

Obviously.

"Indeed?" He skewed one side of his mouth up, and her blush deepened. "About…?"

She fussed with the edge of her serviette, studiously avoiding his gaze.

Bella hopped up and down, trying to climb onto

the chaise and into her owner's lap.

Nicolette picked the puppy up, then notching her chin up an inch, replied, "A book on dog training. Would *you* care to borrow it? I think perhaps you ought to. Sampson could use obedience instruction, I think."

Touché, the little liar.

Booted footsteps echoed on the terrace, and as one, they turned to glance at the far end.

"Ah, Ansley, dear. Do join us," his mother invited with an eager smile. "We have a guest."

"Twice in two days, Westfall?" Scarborough strode forward, his astute indigo gaze assessing, but his countenance expressionless, as it so often was. "Does this mean you intend to court my sister?"

"Ansley, please," Nicolette gently chided, mortification in her gaze. "It's not what you think."

"You might've spoken with me first and saved yourself the effort." His regard shifted to her, and a fond smile bent his mouth. "I'm sorry to disappoint you, Westfall, but she's not interested."

5

Covent Garden

Evening

17 May 1810

Nicolette felt as if every curious eye in the elegant theater was upon her. Her suspicions weren't so very far off. Each time she lifted her attention from the stage and scanned the attendees, she encountered opera glasses blatantly pointed in the direction of Westfall's box.

It was as if a large percentage of those in attendance had no interest at all in the performance but would rather spend the entire time spying on others.

No doubt, speculation ran rampant about the nature of her relationship with Mathias, particularly after several *le beau monde* members had witnessed him carrying her through Hyde Park.

Lord only knew who'd seen him at her house yesterday, too.

And now she sat in his box at the theater.

One plus one plus one equaled courtship in the *bon ton's* mind.

You're doing this for Megan, she reminded herself. *You don't give a pig's farthing what these people think.*

Not *entirely* true.

As much as Nicolette would like to believe that falsehood, she couldn't lie to herself. She *did* care, and it angered and frustrated her that she did.

"They're really quite awful, aren't they?" Mathias's sister, Megan Bridgham, whispered. "Like vultures on carrion."

Yes. Horrid, judgmental hypocrites.

The sweet-faced woman, appearing younger than her seven and twenty years, subtly angled her dark head toward the other patrons' boxes.

"I rather feel like an insect pinned to a board," she confided softly. "I'm tempted to pull a face or stick out my tongue in the manner my sons sometimes do just to shock them."

Nicolette giggled into her hand before saying out the side of her mouth, "I should very much like to see their reactions if you did."

Already, she liked Mathias's sister a good deal.

Megan honestly didn't seem to care a flip for what any of the other theatergoers thought. A pretty woman with dark brown hair rather than midnight like Mathias, she had the same bright blue eyes he possessed. She also had a charming dimple in her left cheek that showed when she smiled, which she did often.

"What are you two whispering about? Should I be concerned?" Westfall's deep voice interjected from behind them. He'd leaned forward so that his breath caressed Nicolette's bare shoulder.

God, help her.

She swallowed and sent her fan in rapid motion,

creating a welcome cooling breeze.

"Nothing of interest to you, dear brother," Megan said smoothly, giving Nicolette's hand a covert squeeze. "Simply an observation about...*insects*."

"*Insects*?" Incredulity leeched into his voice. "Are *we* watching the *same* play, for I definitely do not recall a single mention of an insect of any kind."

"Shh, Mathias," Megan scolded. "You're distracting me, and you know it's been years since I visited the theater."

"*These* insects are swathed in silks, satins, velvets, feathers, and jewels, Your Grace," Nicolette murmured, turning her head slightly to the side to speak to him. "They also have a propensity to wear too much perfume, form unkind opinions, and unabashedly stare."

"*Aah,*" he said, drawing the word out as comprehension dawned. "I see. Did I tell you how lovely you look this evening, Miss Twistleton?"

Again, his warm breath brushed over her skin, and every pore raised in sensual awareness. Why must she be so responsive to him?

"You did, Your Grace."

Twice already.

"Hmm," he murmured into her ear. "Do call me Mathias. You did once before, and I very much liked that."

A frisson of awareness bathed her from her nape to her toes, raising every hair pore in the process even as her bones threatened to turn to jelly.

Goodness, he must stop that.

What would his sister and Nicolette's mother think?

What would all the snoops watching his box think?

Nicolette shook her head. "Indeed, not."

She was having a difficult enough time maintaining a degree of formality and distance between them. Addressing one another by their given-names would not do. Though, when she thought of him, he *was* Mathias and not the duke or his grace. Still, that was her secret, and as long as no one else knew, no harm could come of it.

"Not *yet*," he said in a tone as rich and sweet as

warm chocolate. "But you will, I assure you."

Yes, indeed, she'd melt into a thousand droplets, right here in this box if he kept that up.

Lord, the temperature in the box had become stifling, and Mathias's presence made it all the more difficult to breathe. Nicolette plied her fan faster, and the rotter had the ballocks to chuckle and tug a curl lying over her shoulder.

Why, the scoundrel had done that on purpose, simply to fluster her. Just as he'd asked about her novel yesterday, wicked man.

How could he possibly have known she was reading a gothic romance?

Well, she *had* hidden it beneath her gown, and likely he'd seen her do so.

Even now, searing heat encompassed her at the knowledge, and she refused to contemplate exactly what conclusions he'd drawn from her attempt to conceal the book.

She also studiously ignored the speculative glance Megan slipped her, and the pleased smile bending her mouth. *Bother*. Did she think there was something between Nicolette and her brother?

Naturally, such silly notions must be quashed at once.

Must they?

Mathias was the only man able to get under Nicolette's skin or cause her comportment to slip. Ironically, he was also the only unmarried gentleman she felt genuinely comfortable with besides Ansley. The only one she considered a friend.

Friend?

Her ponderings regarding him most assuredly were not platonic.

Wetting her lips, she fervently wished for something to drink. Her mouth had gone dry as sandpaper when Mathias had whispered in her ear, and she regretted she hadn't worn something a trifle dowdier. Something that wouldn't have him looking at her with that scorching, knowing gaze. Perhaps a grain sack, or a horse blanket, or nun's habit.

Instead, she'd chosen to wear her newest gown. A brilliant, shimmering lawn green masterpiece with a netted overskirt and trimmed in Brussels lace. She'd been quite pleased with her reflection in the cheval mirror except for the amount of décolletage visible above her bodice.

Even now, she resisted laying her palm over the ample cleavage.

Had Madam Lovellette taken it upon herself to alter the neckline to something bordering on scandalous?

Mathias chuckled again before relaxing back into his chair, likely in much the same indolent manner as he had yesterday when Ansley had come upon them.

Dearest Ansley.

Never one to mince words or skirt around an issue, her brother had declared what he believed to be the truth. However, she'd quickly explained Mathias's purpose in visiting was to inveigle them to assist with his sister and not to pay his addresses to Nicolette.

Nonetheless, the conversation had proved remarkably awkward.

Inexplicable disappointment had flooded her, but she resolutely reminded herself that she didn't want any man pursuing her, least of all a peer of the realm such as the Duke of Westfall.

With grim determination, and suspecting Mathias yet watched her and not the performance, she forced her attention back to the actors prancing and orating upon the stage.

Shortly thereafter, intermission was upon them, and they stood to stretch their legs. A footman poured them the iced champagne that had been cooling in a bucket atop a table beside the entrance. As Nicolette sipped the excellent wine, she regarded the throng milling about below.

They presented a colorful, jabbering horde.

A rueful smile bent her mouth as she took another sip. At one time, she'd adored all of this. The routs and balls, the soirées and musicals, the house parties and assemblies.

Now, every time she ventured into public, her behavior was all an act.

A performance, very much like that which they appreciated tonight.

Nicolette had assumed a role, had created a persona to prove to everyone she didn't care a fig that she'd been jilted. That she could still enjoy herself and have a splendid time.

It was a well-orchestrated lie.

She was a sham.

A shiver skittered up Nicolette's spine, raising her nape hairs, and she had the distinct sensation someone watched her. Subtly turning her head, she swept her gaze over the nearby boxes and those across from them and was startled to see a gorgeous, petite blonde attired in a daring scarlet gown, glaring lethal daggers at her.

She actually flinched from the venom speared in her direction.

The gown revealed all but the woman's nipples, and Nicolette marveled at her daring. The diamond and ruby pendant she wore, nestled at the juncture of those generous breasts, drew even the most reticent eye exactly where the woman, no doubt, wanted the regard.

Swiftly averting her attention, Nicolette strove to recall if she'd met the lady before.

She didn't look familiar.

Mathias came to stand beside her, resting one

gloved hand casually on the edge of the box. "Are you enjoying yourself, Nicolette?"

Presumptuous man, using her given name.

She hadn't a doubt he did so to make a point about her not using his.

"I am." She took a sip of champagne, wrinkling her nose as the effervescent bubbles tickled it. "I confess, I'm having as much fun watching people as the performance."

Megan joined them, twining her hand through Nicolette's elbow. She leaned toward Mathias and, in a hushed voice, asked, "Mathias, who is that woman? Almost directly across from us? The one with her— um—endowments spilling from her bodice. She's been sending furious looks in our direction all evening."

Nicolette knitted her eyebrows together.

All evening? Indeed?

Casually lifting his flute, Mathias roved his gaze over the boxes. He stiffened visibly for two heartbeats, his eyelids lowering half-way before he took a swallow of champagne. "That would be Victoria Melbourne,

Viscountess Calbraith," he said slowly.

"Oh. *Oh!*" Megan's eyes widened owlishly before a look of concern replaced her astonishment. Troubling her lower lip, she peeked at the box from beneath her lashes. "Is her husband here, as well?"

Nicolette sensed an undercurrent she couldn't define between the brother and sister.

"No," Mathias said shortly, turning so that his back was to the opening. "He died over a year ago. And like you, Megan, she is only recently out of mourning."

"*Oooh*," Megan said again, her tone most definitely conveying a message Nicolette didn't understand. Megan slid another, considering glance toward the viscountess's box. "Well, this could prove to be *quite* an entertaining evening."

Lifting one eyebrow, she sipped her champagne and returned her focus to her brother.

He shrugged, seemingly disinterested.

Nicolette hadn't met the viscountess, but she was reasonably convinced, given the peculiar exchange between brother and sister, Mathias had. And once he'd identified her, Megan also knew who she was.

"Do you know her, Your Grace?" Nicolette could've bitten her tongue off for blurting the question. Hadn't she just concluded as much?

God above, she didn't sound jealous, did she?

"In a manner of speaking," he murmured, his gaze pointed to the floor.

Megan caught Nicolette's eye and gave an infinitesimal shake of her head while mouthing, "*Later*."

How very peculiar.

Nicolette angled her head in acknowledgment, but couldn't prevent her attention from straying to Mathias again. A pensiveness had crept over his handsome features, and a muscle ticked in his jaw.

Where had the light-hearted duke gone?

She'd never seen this side of Mathias before. He'd always been carefree and jovial, a ready smile on his molded mouth and a blithe compliment on his tongue.

What was going on?

Who was the viscountess to him?

She speared a covert glance to the opposite box to find it empty.

Why did Nicolette care?

For she found she did care, very much indeed.

Foolish girl!

The Duke of Westfall is not for you.

6

Nevertheless, for all of her self-recriminations, Nicolette still couldn't quell the queer lump in her stomach or stop studying Mathias from beneath her eyelashes.

He wore his hair slightly longer than was fashionable, and she supposed some might consider his nose a jot too strong. He possessed high cheekbones, a well-defined chin, and a full, sensual mouth. A most attractive package, she noted, not for the first time.

"I was quite looking forward to visiting with your mother, Your Grace," Mama said, thankfully interrupting the awkward silence that had descended upon the box. Oblivious to the tension, and her face flushed with pleasure, she gazed at him expectantly.

Ever the genial gentleman, Mathias produced one of his disarming smiles and brought his gaze up to hers. "Indeed, Mrs. Twistleton, she was sorry to have to send her regrets. Her megrims are rare, but when one occurs, only a lie down will alleviate her discomfort. She asks that you and Miss Twistleton come for tea on Wednesday if your schedules allow. She'll send an invitation tomorrow."

Eyes shining, Megan squeezed Nicolette's hand. "Oh, do come. I should like you to meet my sons."

"I'd like that very much." Nicolette had felt an immediate affinity for Megan Bridgham and was glad Mathias had asked them to join him tonight.

"I believe she intends to invite several of your close acquaintances as well," Mathias said, pointing his gaze upward as if trying to recall exactly whom. "I'm not sure who, precisely, but the Sutcliffes, Dandridges, Sheffields, and Penningtons, for certain. All people who will warmly welcome Megan into London society."

"My goodness." Megan rolled her eyes, a

mischievous grin curing here mouth. "It's not like it's my Come Out, Mathias."

He caught her hand and fondly kissed the back of it. "Yes, dear sister, but we want to make you feel welcome. Much has changed since you lived here last."

"*Some* things, not so much." Megan's regard slipped to the box opposite theirs, which was now empty of the hostile woman.

"Hmm." He made that throaty noise Nicolette had come to understand was neither an affirmation nor a denial.

However, other than the viscountess's acrimonious glares, the evening had been most pleasurable.

"Tea would be lovely." Mama eyed Mathias from the corner of her eye. A meditative expression creasing her features, she said, "Of course, we shall attend."

Oh, Mama, don't get any ideas. He's just being polite.

A flurry outside their box caught everyone's attention a fraction before the crimson curtain parted, and none other than Lady Calbraith glided in, accompanied by a rather reluctant appearing Lord Crawley.

"Good evening, Your Grace," she purred, dipping into a deep curtsey and giving Mathias a birds-eye view of her ample and very scantily covered décolletage on full display.

Nicolette suppressed a gasp for the tops of the woman's dusky rose areolas were clearly visible above the satin.

"*Oh, my,*" Megan whispered in Nicolette's ear, clearly shocked. She grasped Nicolette's hand as if lending her support. "This cannot be good."

"Viscountess. Crawly." Mathias acknowledged with the barest inclination of his head, his tone neutral.

Nicolette couldn't help the satisfaction curling through her that he hadn't taken a single peek at Lady Calbraith's voluptuous bosom.

He quaffed back the rest of his champagne and held his flute toward the impassive-faced footman who silently accepted the empty glass.

"More, Your Grace?" the servant asked.

"No, thank you." He curved his mouth the merest bit and passed the servant a coin. "You may go."

With an acquiescent dip of his head, the footman departed.

Lady Calbraith pinned her brown-eyed gaze on Nicolette, and despite the upward turn of the slightly older woman's rouged lips, there wasn't an iota of friendliness in her eyes. No, pure venom glittered there, reminding Nicolette of a cobra's predatory gaze.

She had the odd urge to giggle, as an image of herself in her green gown pinned to a display board popped into her head. And then one of Lady Calbraith, those unnaturally perky bosoms sticking out, as she was pinned to a similar board.

Megan squeezed Nicolette's hand again.

Ah, she'd also observed the malevolence in the woman's eyes.

"Aren't you going to introduce us, Westfall?" Lady Calbraith breathed in a husky bedroom voice while coyly fluttering her eyelashes. Well, her voice was what Nicolette imagined a bedroom voice would sound like, in any event.

She almost rolled her eyes at the woman's theatrical performance.

There was no doubt that Lady Calbraith was a practiced flirt. A coquette. And given her choice of gown—which Nicolette strongly suspected she wore nothing beneath—perhaps not so very far removed in station from that of a demimonde.

In truth, women of her ilk did much more than flutter eyelashes and expose vast amounts of breasts. Nicolette wasn't so naive that she didn't recognize a woman of the world. And the viscountess quite obviously had eyes for Mathias.

Something very much like jealousy jabbed Nicolette's ribs.

But that was ridiculous.

She had no claim on Mathias nor he on her.

He sighed, sending Nicolette a look tinged with regret. Or was that shadow deepening his eyes to navy-blue apologetic?

What in the world?

"Oh, there's no need to introduce me to Mrs. and Miss Twistleton," Lord Crawley assured the viscountess, jovially. "We are already well-acquainted." From his slightly slurred speech, he'd imbibed deeply tonight already. "I am not, however, acquainted with *this* young lady."

He all but leered at Megan, in full view of her brother, too.

Mathias flexed his jaw.

He'd perceived as much as well, and for a heartbeat, Nicolette thought he'd refuse the introductions.

Mama coughed delicately behind her hand, a not so subtle hint to get on with it and dispel the expectant, highly charged, atmosphere.

With another pulse of his jaw, Mathias proceeded with the introductions. "Crawley, my sister, *Mrs.* Megan Bridgham." Mathias angled toward his sister and extended an arm. "Megan, Warren, Earl of Crawley."

If Mathias had thought to dissuade the earl's interest by mentioning Megan's marital status—well, former status—he'd made an error in judgment. If anything, the earl's expression became all the more lecherous.

Did he think Megan was the type of married woman who looked for entertainment outside her marriage? Hmm, given his present company, the notion mightn't be so ridiculous.

Crawley was a most apt name, indeed.

He made Nicolette's skin crawl, and from the way Megan had stepped nearer her and tucked her hand into the bend in Nicolette's arm, he did the same to her.

Mathias inclined his dark head toward Lady Calbraith, and an unmistakable chill coloring his tone, stiffly said, "Megan, Mrs. Twistleton, Miss Twistleton, may I introduce Victoria Melbourne, Viscountess Calbraith?"

They all dipped curtsies, and the viscountess fairly preened under the attention.

Nicolette seldom formed an opinion from a first meeting, but she did not like this woman. Not her haughty looks or condescending, superior attitude. The only reason Mama wasn't the Dowager Countess of Scarborough and Nicolette wasn't Lady Nicolette was because Ansley had inherited the earldom from an uncle, rather than his father.

"My lady, my sister Megan Bridgham, Mrs. Mary Twistleton, and Miss Nicolette Twistleton," Mathias finished.

"*Twistleton?* Why do I know that name?" The viscountess arched a perfectly plucked white-blonde eyebrow and made a small *moue* with her rosebud mouth. "Any relation to Ansley Twistleton, Earl of Scarborough?" Lady Calbraith asked, edging closer to Mathias.

Was she serious?

Twistleton wasn't exactly a common name.

"He is my son," Mama said, coolness leaking into her voice and her disapproving stare.

"*Ahh*," Lady Calbraith said before latching onto Mathias's arm. She gave a coy shake of her head. "But that's not where I know the name from." She tapped her chin with her scarlet gloved fingertip, and angling her head in a coquettish manner, gazed up at Mathias. "It will come to me. Let me think."

Mathias appeared more peeved and discomfited than Nicolette had ever seen him.

She finished her champagne and was about to excuse herself to use the lady's retiring room and escape the viscountess's company when Lady Calbraith gave a little artificial laugh. "I have it."

His eyebrows forming a severe line, Mathias scowled at her silvery head, his displeasure tangible.

"You're the chit Kilbourne jilted for the American heiress." She turned her big-eyed, falsely innocent gaze to Nicolette. "The one they call the...*Spiteful Spinster*, yes?"

An outraged gasp escaped Megan, and she promptly wrapped an arm around Nicolette's waist. "What a vicious bitch," she whispered in Nicolette's ear. "Don't mind her."

Nicolette liked Megan all the more for her direct speech.

Mama made a strangled sound, clutching a trembling hand to her throat while sending Nicolette an aghast look. "How dare you?" she seethed, the angriest she'd seen her mother since Kilbourne had callously cast Nicolette aside.

"Now, see here, my lady." Crawley scowled,

looking decidedly uncomfortable. "That was poorly done of you."

"*What?*" Lady Calbraith innocently batted her darkened eyelashes again, affecting a guileless countenance. "I only spoke the truth. She *is* called the *Spiteful Spinster*."

No, she'd meant to sink her talons and draw blood.

Nicolette itched to slap the smugly satisfied look off her painted face.

"Better to be unwed than a whore," Megan whispered in Nicolette's ear.

Nicolette could've hugged her.

Mathias very slowly and very deliberately removed Lady Calbraith's claws from his arm and stepped away from her. He skimmed his contemptuous gaze over her, dismissively, his face hardened into granite planes.

In a voice smooth as silk, but rapier-sharp, he said, "You go too far, Lady Calbraith. But then again, I'm not at all surprised. After all, you and Kilbourne are kindred spirits, are you not?"

Her cherry mouth went slack, and her pansy eyes creased at the corners as she flexed her eyelids in anger.

He faced the other women and made a half-bow. "Please do excuse me. I'll return before the second act. I find I need a bit of fresh air."

Without another word or a backward glance, Mathias strode from the box

"Mathias. Please, wait. You misunderstood." Apparently, realizing she'd overplayed her hand, Lady Calbraith rushed after him, abandoning Lord Crawley altogether.

Mathias?

Oh, Lady Calbraith knew Westfall very well, indeed. What precisely, had he meant that she and Kilbourne were kindred spirits?

Nicolette dropped her focus to the floor as her stomach turned over sickeningly, and she swallowed against the weirdest urge to sob. She did not cry in public, and she assuredly did not weep over men anymore. Because they weren't worth it, and she'd learned that only she was responsible for her happiness and contentment.

Relying on others to fulfill those needs led to disappointment and regrets. And eventually, resentment and bitterness. Which was why Nicolette wasn't entirely undeserving of the unflattering moniker, *Spiteful Spinster*. She *had* become spiteful and vindictive, punishing other men for the Duke of Kilbourne's actions.

Shame and remorse bubbled behind her ribs, expanding ever wider and wider.

"Do excuse me, ladies." His face smattered with red blotches, Lord Crawley pulled at his neckcloth. He sketched a bow and, with great alacrity, scuttled from the box, reminding Nicolette very much of a giant beetle.

Acutely aware this whole debacle might've been witnessed, Nicolette perused the theater. Thank goodness for the intermission for though a few people remained in their boxes and milled about below, Mathias's box wasn't under the scrutiny it had been earlier.

That, however, didn't mean the scene that had just

played out hadn't been witnessed or wouldn't be discussed and speculated upon in London's upper salons tomorrow.

Releasing a long breath through her nose, she pressed a surprisingly cold and unsteady hand to her forehead. And despite her determination otherwise, those old feelings of inadequacy and humiliation assailed her, twisting through her veins.

That...that...*woman.* Oh, Lady Calbraith was simply too odious for words.

"I must say, if I never encounter Lady Calbraith again, it will be too soon," Mama vowed as she plopped onto her chair and began vigorously fanning herself. "I shall give her the cut direct after this and advise my friends to do the same. Of all the nerve. Did you see her gown? I've seen strumpets wearing more."

When had her mother ever seen a strumpet?

Mama sniffed in offended outrage. "'Why buy the cow when you can get the milk for free?' as my grandmama used to say."

Why, indeed?

Nicolette chuckled despite the horridness of the past few minutes.

Her mother had truly forgotten herself.

Raising her eyes, Nicolette met Megan's sympathetic gaze.

"What did Mathias mean, Lady Calbraith and Kilbourne are of the same ilk?" she asked. Nicolette was afraid she already knew, but she needed to hear it, nonetheless.

Megan bit her lip then took both of Nicolette's hands in hers. "She and Mathias became betrothed after I left for India but before he inherited the dukedom. She broke it off and married the viscount. And I believe she regrets her decision, especially now that Mathias is a duke."

Of course, she did.

And that's why Mathias had been so kind to Nicolette.

He knew exactly how she felt.

Megan cut a fretful glance at the parted curtain. "I fear she means to take up where they left off."

Nicolette stared at the box's entrance, the champagne souring in her stomach. Why did the thought make her want to weep?

Mayfair, London

Afternoon

23 May 1810

Mathias was late.

Returning his timepiece to his pocket, he firmed his lips as the carriage rumbled through London's cobbled streets. His mother's tea had started thirty minutes ago, and he'd promised to be present.

He'd taken Nicolette on that coveted ride through Hyde Park in his phaeton, and they'd walked together two mornings. He'd also made a point to attend the Featherspoons' musical, as well as the Middlethorpes' dinner when he'd learned she'd been invited.

They'd developed a camaraderie, and Nicolette no longer attempted to wedge formality between them. Mathias couldn't be more delighted at his purposeful progress.

Two years he'd waited to pursue Nicolette, a woman like no other. She was incomparable, at least in his mind. He wanted very much to be her friend and confidant, someone she could trust without hesitation and rely upon. Hopefully, that trust, friendship, and attraction would grow into something more.

He was a patient man and would wait as long as it took.

Idly flexing his sore hand, Mathias grinned.

By God, his tardiness was worth it, though Mother wouldn't agree.

As he'd made his way through White's, he'd had the unfortunate privilege of encountering the Duke of Kilbourne. The assling, already well into his cups in the middle of the day, had hailed Mathias as he passed by his table.

"Heard you're courting Nicolette Twistleton,

Westfall." He raised his glass, his mouth twisted into a sideways grin. Not much older than Mathias, Kilbourne was one of those dissolute peers who quickly wasted their fortunes on drink, gambling, and whoring. His sedate lifestyle lent to his lily-white hands, soft body, and increasingly fleshy features.

Nicolette was well rid of the whey-faced man, even if she didn't know it.

Mathias had put his sleuthing skills to work and uncovered several unsavory details about Kilbourne.

The duke had managed to blow through a goodly portion of his estranged wife's fortune already. The Duchess of Kilbourne had journeyed to America because he'd beaten her one time too many. She had no plans to return. And Kilbourne had the clap, which was no surprise given his propensity to swive anything in skirts.

"You shouldn't believe everything you hear," Mathias said, nodding politely at the men sitting with Kilbourne, Cliff Preston and Collin Chambers, both younger sons of peers. Also, notorious wastrels.

They returned his nod, boredom etched across

their placid features.

"If you'll excuse me," Mathias said with a dip of his chin. "I have an engagement."

"Come now, no need to be reticent." Kilbourne took a hefty swig of whisky. "By all reports, you carried Nicolette from Hyde Park, and the next day visited her home."

He dared to call her Nicolette after his abominable behavior?

Nicolette with her strength of character? Her gumption and daring? Her loyalty and wit?

Kilbourne's jaded companions perked up at that tidbit.

Lady Darumple had been busy, hadn't the chinwag?

One day, Mathias was going to start an unfathomable rumor within hearing of the woman, a tale so preposterous, only an idiot would believe it. And then he'd sit back and see how swiftly it spread amongst the upper ten thousand.

Perhaps he'd hint Lady Darumple was really a man.

That ought to sort the sensible from the gossipmongers.

"Carried her, *eh*?" Preston said, suggestively before removing his handkerchief from his coat pocket and honking into the cloth with the gusto of a mating gander. "That had to be a tempting armful."

"She's a pretty little partridge, I'll grant you," Chambers agreed, lifting his glass. "But as ill-disposed as an angry scorpion."

Running his square forefinger around the rim of the glass, Kilbourne slouched back in his chair. "And I saw you at the theater together myself last week."

Would he not let the matter go?

A trace of petulance—or was it envy?—tinged his voice as he stared into his drink. "And it's been said you've been seen in each other's company several more times, as well. I'm surprised you have the time given your various *business* enterprises."

He uttered the word with repugnance, as if he chewed rabbit droppings.

Mathias merely skewed a brow, fully accustomed to London Society looking down their aristocratic noses at anyone who actually worked for a living. What bothered him more was why Kilbourne, the rotter, believed he had the right to monitor who Nicolette chose to socialize with.

That assuredly begged an explanation.

"I'd say to anyone's mind, such regular encounters most definitely meet the parameters of courtship," Kilbourne declared, a peeved scowl knitting his eyebrows.

Was he jealous?

Mathias appraised Kilbourne carefully, noting the petulant slant to his weak mouth and the envious glint in his red-rimmed eyes.

Quite possibly.

Ah, that explained much.

The bugger didn't want Nicolette, but he didn't want anyone else to have her either. Despicable cockscum.

Mathias finished donning his other glove before answering in a frosty tone, "If you think I'm discussing Miss Twistleton with you, Kilbourne, you're mistaken."

"I suppose her mother and brother are pressing her to marry. It *has* been over two years," Kilbourne mused, emptying his glass, and plunking it onto the table with a loud bang. "Didn't think she'd *ever* get over me," he said with a smug sideways grin.

What an arrogant bastard.

Kilbourne wasn't fit to wipe Nicolette's feet on.

Mathias's blood surged, but he scratched the side of his nose rather than satisfy his baser instincts and plant Kilbourne the facer he deserved.

"I believe excessive drink has affected your reasoning, Kilbourne. Nicolette Twistleton is an astute, intelligent woman, and she realized long ago, she'd been spared a life of misery when you jilted her." He casually adjusted the cuff of one gray glove. "By the way, *how* is the Duchess of Kilbourne?"

Kilbourne chuckled, nastily. "As frigid as Loch Ness and Nicolette Twistleton. It seems a man can only get a satisfying swive with a whore or an actress."

Mathias balled his fists and forced himself to count to five when what he longed to do was clobber the assling.

I shouldn't.

It will cause a scandal and upset Mother and Nicolette.

Kilbourne's face flushed, and his expression turned belligerent. "Wives might spread their legs before marriage, but as soon as the vows are exchanged, they clamp their thighs together like old maids or virgin nuns. Isn't that right?"

Well pleased with himself at his crude jest, he chuckled again and looked to his friends for confirmation.

As neither was married, they rolled their shoulders, wariness creeping across their faces as they observed Mathias's growing wrath.

Just one punch.

Squarely on his perfectly straight nose.

Mathias counted to five. Then counted to five again.

Think of Mother.

One. Two. Three. Four. Five.

Think of Nicolette.

Think of Megan.

Do not consider how bloody, damn satisfying it would be to knock the sod on his ass.

"Have you managed to thaw the *Spiteful Spinster*, Westfall?" Kilbourne poured another finger's worth of whisky into his glass then cut Mathias a side-eyed glance. "For by God, the prude never permitted me more than a chaste kiss upon the cheek during our betrothal. Was it any wonder I found release elsewhere?"

Two punches.

One on the nose and another to shut his gob.

"Kilbourne?"

The duke turned his flushed, slightly puffy face to Mathias.

"What?" he asked insolently.

Mathias bent down and whispered into his ear. "If I ever hear Nicolette Twistleton's name on your foul tongue again, or if I hear the smallest snippet of gossip about her that originated from you, you *will* answer to me."

"I thought you weren't courting the chit," Kilbourne scoffed. The edges of his eyes crinkled, and a shrewd glint entered his bloodshot gaze. "Or...*have* you had more success bedding the chit than I did? There are bets on the books that you have, but I didn't give them any credit. I'd never taken Nicolette for a promiscuous strumpet."

Christ and all of the saints, give me strength and lots of it

Mathias closed his eyes for a heartbeat struggling to corral his swiftly burgeoning temper.

Had people nothing better to do than wager on something so vulgar and demeaning as Nicolette's virtue?

"I might have to place a wager myself now," Kilbourne muttered conversationally as if they discussed the latest racehorse the Duke of Waycross had purchased at Tattersall's

One, two, three—oh, to hell with it.

Mathias had Kilbourne by the cravat and out of his chair in a heartbeat. "I did warn you."

He let go with a punch that sent the duke soaring backward and crashing into the table, sending the glasses and whisky bottle flying. Glass shattered, the table splintered, and conversations abruptly ceased.

Kilbourne crumpled to the floor, blood oozing from his split lip. Raising up on one elbow, he gingerly touched his mouth, his infuriated gaze spewing hatred.

"How dare you?" he seethed, eyeing his reddened fingertips.

One punch, it is then.

Preston and Chambers had both scrambled out of the way like a pair of frightened roosters. But now Chambers ventured forth and offered Kilbourne a handkerchief and a hand up.

Leveling Mathias a murderous glare, Kilbourne gained his feet. He spat a mouthful of blood onto the gleaming wood floor. "You'll pay for this, Westfall."

Hardly.

Men of Kilbourne's ilk were all bluster and no ballocks.

"That's only a taste of what I'll do to you. You'd be wise to remember that." Mathias had promptly spun on his heel and left because the urge to beat Kilbourne to a pulp for besmirching Nicolette was so great, he didn't trust himself.

Besides, he'd have a hard time explaining his disheveled state to his mother's guests, and he'd save Nicolette the humiliation of ever knowing what had taken place. Although, in truth, with all of the witnesses present, what had occurred would likely leak out.

He could only hope that she'd not hear of it.

As the carriage trundled along, Mathias flexed his fingers again, testing each digit in turn.

He'd bruised his knuckles, but none were broken.

In all probability, he'd be expelled from White's for a time. But by damn, he'd punch Kilbourne again. Only next time, he'd get *both* face plants in.

Did Nicolette know how fortunate she was to be rid of that whoremongering cockscum?

A few minutes later, the carriage lumbered to a stop outside his house. He alighted and greeted his butler as he ascended the steps. "Good afternoon, Selby."

"Your Grace." Selby shut the door behind Mathias then accepted his hat.

"Can I presume everyone has arrived already?"

Mathias asked, eyeing the corridor leading to the drawing room.

"Indeed, Your Grace." Selby's too perceptive gaze sank to Mathias's glove, noting the bloodstain across the knuckles. "Might I presume to suggest a change of gloves are in order?"

"Indeed. Please inform my mother I've arrived home. Extend my apologies for my tardiness and beg her indulgence for a few more minutes."

The butler's benign gaze drifted to the bloodied glove again. "I deduce as you've no bruises or cuts that the—*ah*—encounter was short-lived?"

"Indeed." Mathias grinned and winked. "One punch."

Selby quirked a brow, the merest shred of approval slanting his mouth. "Well done, Your Grace."

"Let my mother know, will you?" Mathias didn't wait for the butler's affirmation.

Running up the stairs, he peeled his gloves off, feeling oddly invigorated. It had felt damn good to defend Nicolette. Her family had done an admirable job of protecting her. But no one had stood up to that bastard Kilbourne or confronted him for his ill-treatment of her.

In all likelihood, she'd forbidden her brother to confront him for fear he'd call Kilbourne out. Scarborough was no coward, but he adored his sister. He'd likely not wanted to distress her further.

A few minutes later, wearing clean gloves, Mathias entered the drawing room. He paused at the entrance to locate Nicolette. He spied her almost at once and permitted himself the indulgence of watching her for a few moments.

His heart swelled, emotion—*nay love*—straining against his ribs.

These feelings that he'd forbidden free reign for so long, now sprang forth unbidden and burgeoned into full bloom. Because, at last, he truly believed he might—just might—win this remarkable, exceptional woman's regard, and perhaps, someday, her heart.

She sat chatting with a very pregnant Theadosia, Duchess of Sutcliffe, Justina Farthington, his sister, and Jemmah, Duchess of Dandridge. They laughed over something Theadosia said as she patted her rounded tummy, and his heart quickened at the joy blossoming across Nicolette's face.

What he would give to see her that happy always.

Tearing his attention from Nicolette, he inspected the room.

Mother had outdone herself.

Even her beloved Pomeranians were nowhere to be seen.

If there were fewer than thirty of the most influential *haut ton* elite here, he'd forgo brandy for a fortnight—a sacrifice, indeed. How she'd managed it in less than a week, he couldn't conceive. Several other members of The Sinful Lord's Secret Society were also present, though now that many of the peers were married, they weren't nearly as sinful.

Nicolette glanced up at that moment, and across the distance, their gazes meshed and held.

Dark blue melding with cornflower blue.

As he strode directly to her, he couldn't break the provocative connection, even though it was sure to garner attention and provoke conjecture.

Mathias didn't bloody well care. His heart and

soul hummed with excitement.

He supposed he must've acknowledged the greetings sent his way; after all, his closest friends were here, but he didn't recall doing so.

His entire focus was on Nicolette.

She drew him to her like a magnet to steel or the pull of ocean waves to the shore. Neither had any control over the forces that compelled them together.

Becoming pink tinted her cheeks, but she didn't look away, either.

Brave darling.

She'd never affected coyness or diffidence with him. Only honesty and genuineness, as pure as her soul. Utterly exquisite in an ice-blue gown, which made her ivory skin glow and her blue eyes sparkle, a soft smile bent her pink mouth.

Mathias bowed before her. "Miss Twistleton."

"Your Grace."

"I trust the books I had delivered, met with your approval," he said with a teasing grin.

The other afternoon, when he'd been in Piccadilly for a business meeting, he'd found himself wandering into Hatchard's, of all places. What was more, he'd asked the clerk to discreetly gather five romance novels that were most popular with young ladies.

With a knowing dip of his head, the diminutive man had returned five minutes later, wrapped the books in nondescript brown paper, and tied the bundle with a string.

Mathias had paid for the volumes and gave the clerk Nicolette's direction. "May I borrow a pen?" he asked, withdrawing one of his cards.

"Of course, Your Grace." The eager clerk had produced a quill and ink.

Mathias pondered for a moment before putting the nib to the card.

I hope you find these more diverting than publications about dog training.

With warm regard,

Westfall

His actions were, in truth, beyond the pale, but somehow, he knew Nicolette wouldn't be offended, but rather, pleased at the gesture.

Looking at her now, the color blossoming across her cheeks, he knew he'd been correct in that assumption.

"They did, and they proved most—diverting." Nicolette angled her head. "Thank you."

They continued staring at each other until Megan cleared her throat. "Mathias?"

With a start, he pulled himself together and greeted the other women, all too aware of the knowing glances they exchanged.

Good. The sooner word spread that Mathias had more than a passing interest in Nicolette Twistleton, the better.

"Darling, you're late," his Mother chastised, approaching him and offering her powdered cheek.

He kissed the soft skin, breathing in her lemon and verbena fragrance. "Do forgive me, Mother. I regret something unavoidable detained me."

"Of course, dearest." Bending her mouth into a tolerant smile, she patted his forearm. "Selby explained that an urgent humanitarian issue delayed you. So like you to attend to another's needs before your own."

Humanitarian—?

Oh.

God, love him. Selby was brilliant. Mathias made a mental note to increase the majordomo's wages.

Everleigh, the Duchess of Sheffield crossed to them on her husband's arm. "Griffin and I were just discussing our ball next week with your mother, Westfall. We do hope you will attend."

After the scandal involving Crispin, Duke of Bainbridge, and Jessica Brentwood at the ball Mathias and his mother had hosted in late April, he'd sworn off attending or holding balls this Season. Or next. Or ever, for that matter.

However, that debacle had unexpectedly ended rather well. Bainbridge had married Jessica, the woman he'd secretly been in love with for years, and the two were presently enjoying their wedding trip.

He could well empathize with his friend, who'd harbored a secret affection in much the same manner Mathias had. The major difference was that Jessica Brentwood, unlike Nicolette, didn't eschew and eviscerate anything with trousers that dared to show her more than passing interest.

Glancing at Nicolette from beneath half-lowered lids, Mathias impulsively decided now was as good time as any to make his intentions formally known. He did, in truth, mean to court the enigmatic *Spiteful Spinster*. If only others knew her the way he did, men would be clamoring to make her their wife.

He wasn't entirely positive when he'd made the decision. It was almost as if it had developed on its own after he'd held Nicolette in his arms, and deciding she should be his wife felt as right as anything ever had.

What Mathias did know was that he loved her, wanted to see her smile, and her eyes glow with joy, wanted to hear her brilliant witticisms, and wanted to be the man who healed her heart and spirit.

He didn't doubt he could do that if she'd allow him to.

Bending his mouth into his most charming smile, he answered her grace. "Only if Miss Twistleton agrees to save me a dance. Or two."

His mother threw him a dumbfounded glance before she turned her keen regard to Nicolette. Was that a pleased smile teasing the corners of Mother's mouth?

In an instant, he realized his colossal mistake in essentially publicly declaring himself.

Nicolette stiffened her spine and clasped her hands so tightly, the knuckles turned white. Her practiced mask of indifference slipped into place, transforming her right before his eyes. She fashioned one of her insincere smiles, and his heart plummeted to his feet like a millstone.

Ah, hell.

"Ah, but, Your Grace," she murmured. "I *never* dance with a duke."

8

The Duke and Duchess of Sheffield's Ball
1 June 1810

Surrounded by several of her friends, Nicolette laughed at Sophronie Slater's retelling of the first time she'd ridden astride.

"I could scarcely walk for a week, so chaffed were my thighs," the American said, between giggles, revealing her slightly crooked front teeth. "The next time, I wore special, soft leather trousers I had made just for the occasion, much to my dear papa's chagrin. He says the practice of a female riding astride is too masculine."

"I've never ridden astride," Nicolette confessed. "Though I've always wanted to try. I have trained with weapons, however, and admit I quite like fencing. I'm not as fond of firing a gun. It does rather ruin one's gloves."

Those, too, were considered masculine undertakings.

Nevertheless, she and a few of her friends had taken it upon themselves to learn shooting and fencing, and even how to throw a dagger with considerable accuracy. In truth, more as a means of self-defense than anything else.

For all of her mother's desire to see her happily married, she'd never forbid Nicolette the unusual training in weaponry. Mama also balked at the constraints put on women by men—some well-meaning and others merely controlling.

Somehow, Nicolette didn't think Mathias would be appalled if he learned she could wield a blade and shoot a pistol. No, in fact, she thought he might well applaud.

"I have ridden astride. Quite frequently,"

Gabriella, the Duchess of Pennington, admitted quietly.

Raised by very strict grandparents, Gabriella's announcement took Nicolette by surprise and given the other women's equally flabbergasted expressions, them as well.

Gabriella looked around guardedly to see who might be listening. Satisfied, no one earwigged on their conversation, she said, "Roni is absolutely correct. Once you've done so, you truly dislike riding side-saddle. There's so much more freedom astride."

"Gabby, I didn't know you had," her sister Ophelia Brentwood chided in astonishment. "You sly chit you. How could you keep that from me?"

Gabriella looped her arm through her sister's elbow. "Darling, you know perfectly well our grandparents would've had a conniption, and I didn't want you reprimanded."

"Hmph. Well, I fully intend to join Roni tomorrow, just so you know." Ophelia puckered her forehead as she fluttered her fan. "Although what I'll use to cover my legs, I'm not sure." She gave her sister an intense look. "What did you use, Gabby?"

"I wore multiple pantalettes."

Although not strictly in fashion, more and more women were wearing the undergarment.

Nicolette tilted her head. "I should very much like to join you tomorrow, as well."

In truth, it sounded like great fun, and the slightly scandalous aspect appealed greatly.

Mayhap she could borrow a pair of Ansley's trousers, for Mama wasn't of the mind pantalettes were a necessity. However, the next time Nicolette visited the modiste, she meant to have a pair of riding britches made. And when they repaired to Fawtonbrooke Hall for the summer, she fully intended to pursue riding astride.

My, swearing and riding astride. She was indeed becoming a pariah.

"I've never ridden a horse astride, but I have ridden an elephant and a camel." Megan crinkled her nose. "Trust me. A horse smells much better, and they don't spit."

"How marvelous." Nicolette grinned at Megan.

"An elephant *and* a camel? Was it thrilling?"

Chuckling, Megan nodded. "The elephant, yes. Not so much the camel. They urinate on their legs and the stench..."

She pinched her nose and crossed her eyes.

Her silliness pitched them into a fit of giggles.

Nicolette liked Mathias's sister. A great deal, truth to tell.

At the tea last week, she'd met Megan's three dark-eyed boys. Timothy, the eldest at seven, was a solemn little chap with missing front teeth. He resembled his mother a great deal. However, six-year-old Eric and four-year-old Gregory both sported shocks of red hair. Their father's hair, Megan had explained, a faraway look in her misty, blue eyes.

That she still grieved for her beloved husband was obvious.

At one time, Nicolette had believed she'd wanted that kind of love.

You still do.

Pressing her lips together, she admitted to herself, she'd never loved Kilbourne in that way. Oh, she'd held him in fond regard, but he hadn't invaded her thoughts during the day and her dreams at night. There'd never been an overwhelming urge to kiss him, much less have him touch her in the ways she'd daydreamed about Mathias caressing her.

She couldn't even recall how Kilbourne smelled, but she did remember his perpetually foul breath—a combination of rotten eggs, garlic, and cigars.

A most noxious mixture.

But—and this was most worrisome—Nicolette knew *exactly* how Mathias smelled: peppermint, soap and starch, and sandalwood. Sometimes a hint of brandy or horse or leather, too. And *he* did invade her thoughts, very much as he did at this precise moment.

She'd looked forward to every outing with him. Every conversation, every secretive glance, every unintentional touch.

Just contemplating the latter sent a scorching flush over her entire body, made her breasts heavy, and caused an unsettling ache to coil low in her belly.

"We shall have a grand time."

Sophronie's excited declaration reined in

Nicolette's reveries and brought her back to the present. This tendency to woolgather had never beset her before, and it was most discomposing.

Sophronie grinned, her blue-green eyes flashing with a combination of mischief and excitement. "Meet me in Hyde Park tomorrow morning, at half of eight before everyone is out and about. I'll bring two docile mounts."

Wise that.

Most of the *ton* didn't venture from their plush mattresses until mid-morning at the earliest. Nicolette would need to depart for home soon if she were to arise early enough in the morn. She rarely stayed until a ball ended, in any event, so no one would take notice if she departed a trifle earlier than usual.

Hopefully, Mama wouldn't object.

"Everyone who wants a chance is welcome. And we can always meet again." Sophronie glanced around the circle of women to include them. "Do try to find yourself a pair of pantaloons or extra thick small clothes. Or, you may do as the duchess did and wear multiple layers of garments. Also, be prepared for your thighs to be somewhat tender afterward."

"I think I shall go," Justina Farthington said with the merest hint of defiance in her pale green eyes. "I've decided of late to take risks, and this is a good place to start."

Justina never did anything the least bit untoward, and for her to declare her intention to participate was quite something, indeed.

"Roni?" said Everleigh, Duchess of Sheffield. "Griffin mentioned that you've actually ridden your thoroughbreds in races. That's so exciting and daring."

"No, I've only raced them during training exercises." Sophronie shook her head, causing the strawberry blonde curls framing her face to bounce. She pulled her mouth into a slightly vexed grimace. "Women aren't allowed to actually ride for competition in America, any more than they are permitted to do so here. Rather ridiculous if you ask me. Particularly since not a single male jockey has been able to beat my time. I know I would've won races had I been permitted to compete."

That brought several murmurs of approval.

Unlike the American heiress Maribelle Grosenick, Sophronie wasn't cold and unapproachable or full of her own self import. The petite girl was, however, rather like a dervish, brimming with exuberance and enthusiasm, and one found oneself quite out of breath in her presence.

"I agree. It does seem unfair." Her amber-brown eyes full of understanding, Rayne Westbrook gave Sophronie a sympathetic smile.

Everleigh sniffed. "Hmph. Men claim *we* are the weaker sex, but I'd like to see a single one of them give birth.

That declaration met with uproarious mirth.

"There you are, my dear." Victor, Duke of Sutcliffe, accompanied by Maxwell, Duke of Pennington, and Baxter, Duke of San Sebastian, approached. Two other men accompanied them, but Nicolette wasn't familiar with either.

Notably absent was the Duke of Westfall.

A prick of disappointment jabbed her.

Her flippant response to his jest about a dance or two tonight had fallen flat, and he'd excused himself immediately afterward.

She hadn't seen him since, and she'd missed him dreadfully. Missed their outings and conversations. Missed the comfortable camaraderie between them. Pray God, she hadn't ruined everything with her thoughtless words.

Though it hadn't been her intent, she'd offended Mathias. Every instinct of self-preservation had surged forward, and she'd said the first glib thing which had sprung to mind.

However, she hadn't lied.

Yes, she danced at gatherings, but very infrequently. And she hadn't danced with a duke since Kilbourne's treachery. She supposed it was part of the unwritten rules she'd created to protect herself from ever being in the same degrading circumstance again.

Turned out in their evening finery, the gentlemen who'd joined them presented quite an impressive array of masculine virility. *The ducal assemblage, again.*

Sutcliffe swiftly performed introductions, no small feat considering how many people were clustered together. The two newcomers were both Scots: Evan

Gordonstone, Duke of Waycross, and Fletcher McQuinton, Duke of Kincade.

The first discordant chords of a waltz sounded, and Pennington claimed his wife for the dance. "Duchess, join me for a dance."

Gabriella placed her hand in his before saying, "I look forward to tomorrow, ladies."

"What's happening tomorrow?" he asked as he led her away.

"Oh, just a little get together we ladies spontaneously decided upon," she replied offhandedly.

Even daring Gabriella wasn't quite prepared to share their upcoming adventure with her beloved husband.

As the others partnered off, Nicolette excused herself as was her wont, though she wasn't the type to disappear into a library or study for the duration. Honestly, she enjoyed the gatherings and assemblies if there wasn't always the pressure to find a husband.

And for those who chose not to, or who were wallflowers or spinsters on the shelf, there was always the public disappointment of having failed the two things expected of every woman: to marry and have children.

She wandered the ballroom's periphery, noting with interest that one of the Scottish dukes partnered Sophronie. She didn't look the least pleased about the conversation they were having. Looking smart in his red and white uniform, a lieutenant whirled a rather dazed Rayne around the dance floor.

Nicolette had just reached the open French windows and was considering whether she should risk stepping outside for a breath of fresh air without an escort when a familiar voice rumbled behind her.

"Waltz with me, Nicolette. Please."

She closed her eyes against the tingles rippling up her back and across her shoulder. If Mathias's voice caused this reaction, what would being in his arms again do to her?

"I…"

Taking her elbow, he turned her toward him. "It's just a dance."

Is that really all it is?

She looked into his eyes, and what she saw there

both thrilled and scared her.

He desired her.

And God help her, she wanted him, too.

Swallowing, she took in the colorful tapestry of swirling dancers. The mirrored walls reflected the bright gowns and jewels as a thousand candles lent a warm, almost ethereal glow.

"If your ankle is completely healed, that is." Hope and anticipation made his voice slightly rough around the edges.

"All right," she conceded.

She wanted this. Yearned to dance with Mathias and feel his arms around her, much, *much* more than she ought to. Placing her hand in his, the now-familiar tremor of awareness curled through her in warm, sensual waves.

It had never been like this with Kilbourne. *Never.*

Nicolette very much feared she might regret this later, but she also feared she'd regret even more not dancing with Mathias. Against her will and common sense, she'd somehow become smitten with him.

More than smitten. Wholly and utterly besotted, in

truth. Perhaps…more.

And every minute she spent with him reinforced the emotion. A feeling she'd thought she'd locked away for good. But, in truth, she'd never experienced it in its marvelous complexity and all-encompassing exhilaration until him.

If she thought Kilbourne's rejection had wounded, the loss of Mathias would eviscerate her. There would be no façade of bravado and thumbing her nose at society for whispering behind her back. No more ignoring the *Spiteful Spinster* taunts.

For what she'd felt for Alfonse, Duke of Kilbourne didn't begin to compare to this mesmerizing sentiment that had ensnared her. It was as disparate as a typhoon to a summer breeze or the ocean to a puddle.

Nicolette reveled at the sensation of her palm cradled in Mathias's, and the warmth permeating his eyes stirred an answering reaction in her. When he placed his hand at her waist, she had to resist the overwhelming urge to step closer. And closer still, until nothing but fabric separated them.

And even that was too much.

Way too much.

How could this be?

How could the heat of his hand cradling her ribs, cause such a rush of scorching heat? She fully expected to see a handprint on her skin when she disrobed tonight.

She'd been acquainted with Mathias for years, so why of a sudden did he matter more than anything or anyone else?

Because she'd always kept him at a distance, treated him with formality and coolness until that fateful day in the park. And once she'd permitted him inside, relinquished her guard, he'd subtly invaded every nuance of her life. And she didn't mind—wasn't afraid anymore.

He held his gaze upon her face, unwaveringly. She knew, for her focus remained fixated on him as well.

Good heavens.

This was just like something from the romance novel she'd finished last night. *A Not so Sensible Thing* had been the third book she'd read that Mathias had gifted her, and she'd sighed when she'd read the last page.

Scrambling around for something to talk about, she said, "Did you know Megan has ridden an elephant and a camel?"

"And do you wish to ride such exotic creatures?" Humor danced in Mathias's eyes as if he knew how much he rattled her composure.

"An elephant, most definitely, but I'm not positive about camels. Megan says they spit."

"An African elephant or Asian elephant?" His words spilled over her, heightening each sense to painful awareness.

How could he possibly make speaking about pachyderms be a sensual experience?

"Oh, both, I should think."

"Hmm." He made that low humming in his throat, and another wave of desire crested over her.

"You're staring, Mathias."

"I know."

A thrill jolted through Nicolette. She licked her lips, and his mouth curved the merest bit upward.

"People will notice," she murmured, lowering her

regard to his firm mouth.

How could a man's mouth be so captivating?

And why, above all else, did she yearn to feel those lips upon hers?

"I know that, too." He rolled his shoulder the merest bit. "And I cannot bring myself to care one jot."

Her heartbeat and pulse accelerated at his admission.

Could he possibly feel what she did?

At last, she averted her gaze, focusing instead on his jacket lapel. "But I do, Mathias, as much as I loathe to admit it. I've borne their harsh, unforgiving scrutiny for so long."

She peeked at him.

With an affectionate smile that made her silly heart flop behind her breastbone, he shifted his attention to her mouth.

"Now *you're* staring at *my* mouth," she said, her voice husky and throaty.

Good heavens, she sounded as wanton as Lady Calbraith.

"Because, at this moment, my darling, there is

nothing I long for more than to kiss you." He brought his mouth close to her ear. "To taste your sweet lips and explore your honeyed mouth with my tongue. To start."

Nicolette's heart skipped a beat then resumed beating at twice it's normal rhythm.

God above.

His gravelly timbre had her ready to dissolve into a molten puddle on the sanded floor.

She missed a step, but he caught her, speedily setting her to the right cadence once more.

"Easy, darling," he whispered, his warm breath wisping across her ear, full of sensual promise.

The image he conjured, describing how he wanted to kiss her clouded her vision, and God help her—she wanted that, too.

Nicolette had never been properly kissed. Not in

the fashion Mathias had so eloquently, so erotically, described.

All too soon, the waltz came to an end, the music fading, and she dimly realized they were near where they'd started. Before the magic of the dance and the moment had swept them away to a different time and place.

And still, they stood hands entwined, her palm upon his shoulder and his at her waist.

A nearby male coughed discreetly. "Westfall."

What?

"Ahem." The man loudly cleared his throat.

Nicolette struggled to gather her scattered wits and focus on her surroundings.

Mathias cut an impatient glance to his left, where the Duke of Sutcliffe regarded him with a faintly amused expression on his face.

The spell shattered, and with a jerk, Nicolette stepped away, blushing furiously.

Lord.

She couldn't bear to look around and see who stared, who had seen her acting the love-struck ninny.

"Please excuse me."

Her gaze pointed to the ground, Nicolette swept onto the terrace, her only thought, to escape their scrutiny. Once out of sight of the ballroom, she released a huge pent-up breath then gulped in another of the bracing night air. And another.

Her head swam with a heady giddiness, sensual awareness, and, yes, the slightest iota of fear.

What, pray God, had just happened?

A tidal wave of emotion bludgeoned Nicolette.

She loved Mathias.

A tear squeezed its way out the corner of her eye and trailed down her cheek. She swiped it away, but another took its place.

Desperate, afraid someone would come upon her, she fled into the garden.

Lanterns and torches lit the tidy pathways and wrought-iron benches, creating a whimsical fairyland. She turned down one path and then another until she came to a fountain burbling in the center of a paved circle bordered by a quartet of stone benches. Statues of Greek gods and goddesses stood at attention between each ornate bench, their sightless eyes staring into the night.

The sweet, subtle fragrances of jasmine, peonies, roses, and several other early summer blossoms wafted by, adding to the enchanting atmosphere

Sinking onto the nearest bench between Apollo and Aphrodite, she put her fist to her mouth to curb her lower lip's trembling.

Oh, God.

Nicolette didn't know how it had happened, but she'd not been diligent enough, after all. Her guard had faltered. And somehow, Mathias, Duke of Westfall, had slipped behind her buttresses and had laid claim to her heart.

She loved him.

And not the schoolgirl infatuation she'd felt for Kilbourne.

No, this sentiment was a living, breathing, hypnotic maelstrom that commandeered every aspect of her. *This* was love. Real love. The kind she'd always dreamed of and had stopped believing in.

"Nicolette?" Mathias's silky-smooth timber

caressed her. "Darling, are you all right? You fled before I could speak with you."

His smile was endearingly bashful. Charmingly vulnerable. And if she hadn't already been in love with him, she'd have fallen in love at that moment.

She averted her face and shook her head. Struggling to regain her composure, she said, "I just needed a moment."

A moment to come to grips with my love for you.

He sank onto the bench beside her, his heat enveloping her at once. Without a word, he drew her back against his chest and pressed a kiss to her crown. "Forgive me if I overstepped. I seem to forget myself when I'm with you. I'm completely under your spell, Nicolette."

A watery chuckle escaped her. "And I with you."

Whenever she was in his arms, the world felt right.

Relaxing into Mathias's sturdy strength, she angled her head, looking up at the sky. Though it was a cloudless night, few stars were visible because of London's many lights, and the new moon wasn't noticeable at all.

With one finger, he turned her chin toward him, their eyes meeting.

Searching. Seeking. Speaking what neither had dared to voice.

And call her a fool, Nicolette closed her eyes and raised her mouth. Silently inviting him to give her what she craved, more than oxygen or food or water.

Not a heartbeat later, he settled those marvelous lips upon hers.

And he did everything he'd promised during that tantalizing dance, and more.

So much more.

She turned into Mathias, sliding her arms around his back and clutching him to her, letting sensation and desire take over.

"Nicolette, my sweet darling." He groaned low in his throat, and a thrill shot through her that she'd brought him to this state.

He kissed the sensitive place below her ear, and she angled her head to allow him better access. Who knew a kiss in that particular spot could pebble her nipples and cause dampness to gather in the cleft between her legs?

In this blissful moment, she didn't care that this was unwise.

Perhaps, utterly foolish.

That it might lead to heartache and regrets.

I love him. I love him. I love Mathias.

She craved Mathias's kisses. Wanted his embrace and wanted to feel his muscles bunching and flexing beneath her palms.

"Permit me to call on your brother tomorrow," he whispered into her ear.

That brought reality crashing down upon her, and she drew back, that old uncertainty and fear assailing her as she searched his face.

"Why?"

To ask for her hand?

A merciless vise clamped her heart.

Yes... No... Yes.

How could she concurrently long for something and yet be utterly terrified of that very thing?

Mathias's raven eyebrows flexed into a

momentary frown before his face cleared.

"Nicolette, you don't think I'd kiss you like this if my intentions were not honorable?" He lifted her hand and pressed firm, warm lips to the inside of her wrist. "I wish to pay my addresses, to court you, and if you are agreeable, make you my duchess, because I—"

"Well, isn't *this* cozy?" drawled a droll, sardonic voice.

Her former betrothed.

God, why now?

A chill skated down Nicolette's spine, and she clutched Mathias's hand. Shutting her eyes, she dragged in a calming breath.

She made to pull away, but Mathias held her firm. "Let me handle this," he murmured.

Giving a tight nod, she glanced over his shoulder.

A yellow-green bruise and a healing cut on his lower lip revealed Kilbourne had been in a fight recently.

"Who knew the *Spiteful Spinster*, Nicolette Twistleton, was really a little trollop?" Kilbourne sneered, slurring his words.

Nicolette's stomach coiled, and she couldn't quite prevent her upper lip from curling.

What a dissolute sot.

Though she'd experienced heartache and disappointment, she also recognized she'd been spared far worse when he'd jilted her. Thank God he had, or she'd never have known unconditional love.

"Have a care, Kilbourne," Mathias said, an unmistakable steely thread to his words as he stood and drew Nicolette to her feet. "I expressly made my feelings on the matter clear, previously. Besmirch Nicolette again, and we will face each other on a dueling field."

"No, Mathias. You cannot," she gasped, clasping his forearm. Tugging on his arm, she said, "Let's return inside. Please."

Kilbourne wasn't worth being injured or dying over.

That's what she'd told Ansley when he vowed to meet the duke on the field of honor after he'd jilted Nicolette. She'd pleaded with him and told her brother she loved him too much for him to take such a risk.

And now, here was Mathias threatening that very thing. A wave of dizziness swirled through her at the thought of him being taken from her. She could not face life without him. Not when she'd just realized how very precious he was to her.

She'd read about such fanciful notions in her novels and had always attributed that nonsense to the heroines' overwrought emotions. But this terror frantically tunneling through her was all too real.

Kilbourne's insults mattered not.

Her reputation mattered not.

All that *did* matter was Mathias's safety.

Yes, I recall, Westfall." Kilbourne touched his mouth with a gloved finger. "You punched me for calling her promiscuous."

Mathias had?

When?

"But this…" Kilbourne waved a languid hand toward them, wavering unsteadily on his feet. "Proves I was right in my assumptions. After you left White's, I bet twenty pounds, you'd bedded her already."

What a loathsome wretch.

He gave them a sloppy grin. "Seems I won that wager."

Mathias went impossibly still before grating out, his voice dangerously low and lethal, "I warned you, Kilbourne. Now I shall demand satisfaction."

"No, Mathias," Nicolette protested, digging her fingertips into his arm. "I don't care what he says or thinks. He is nobody. Nothing."

Kilbourne looked slightly taken aback.

Conceited bore.

Did he really think she'd been pining over *him* for all of these months?

"But, I do," Mathias said, a hint of something lethal in his silky tone.

"Because I called *her* a trollop? Or was it, strumpet?" Kilbourn threw his head back and laughed. "Nicolette's behavior tonight proves that I was right."

"It's Miss Twistleton to you, and a man has the right to kiss his betrothed, Kilbourne, as you well know."

Betrothed?

Nicolette choked on another gasp and shot her

gaze to Mathias's face, her eyes roving over his features, trying to discern if he jested. And if he wasn't...

She closed her eyes for an instant, the implications of his declaration cascading over her.

Instead of anger at his high-handedness, a delicious warmth started in her center and spiraled outward in divine waves.

Mathias was protecting her, claiming her as his own.

And she found she didn't mind at all. It thrilled her on a primal level and riled a fury toward Kilbourne she'd long held suppressed.

"Hmm, Your Grace." Nicolette angled her chin upward in defiance and went on the offensive. She curved her mouth into an icy smile. "*You* are ridiculing me? Rather the pot calling the kettle black." Arching an imperious brow, she murmured speculatively, "I wonder which of those foul terms do you use for *your* wife since the evidence of her and your *indiscretion* arrived a mere six months after you and she wed?"

His eyes bugging out in disbelief at her

brazenness, Kilbourne made a choking sound.

Not feeling the least remorseful about her appalling forwardness, Nicolette merely smiled sweetly.

Mathias didn't spare her a glance but kept his irate focus trained on the other man. Mathias's jaw flexed, and his nostrils quivered with suppressed rage. "I shall meet you on the field of honor, do not doubt it."

A grayish-green tint to his features, Kilbourne looked decidedly ill, a sheen of sweat popping out on his forehead. Likely the duke believed he could insult her, bandy her good name about, and suffer no more repercussions than he had when he'd left her at the altar.

Except, Mathias was a duke, an equal to Kilbourne, and he could demand retribution.

"Sutcliffe and Pennington will act as my seconds." Mathias clipped out each word, a snap of controlled fury. "Name your seconds and pick your weapon. I'll see you at dawn the day after tomorrow."

"Oh, Mathias," Nicolette whispered. "No."

The severity of the situation dismantled her prior

satisfaction.

Kilbourne slanted her a baffled glance before giving a stiff jerk of his head. "As you wish."

"And Kilbourne," Mathias continued in a conversational tone. "Do consider carefully what you tell others when you go inside. It may very well make a difference whether I only draw first blood or end your miserable life."

The temperate calm with which Mathias delivered that threat sent a shiver scuttling down Nicolette's spine and raised her nape hair.

My God. He's deadly serious.

His pallor waxen, Kilbourne stomped off without another word, his drunken gait uneven.

"Come, sweetheart. We should return to the ballroom." Mathias tucked Nicolette's hand into his arm. He was silent as they made the return trip along the well-tended pathways.

Nicolette's mind whirled around and around, replaying what had just occurred and then leaping foreword to the day after tomorrow. To the duel. She must stop this insanity.

Tremors rippled through her as he slowly guided her back to the house. It wasn't fear for her reputation, but stark terror for Mathias that sent shudder after shudder pulsing through her.

"Mathias, you cannot fight a duel over a drunken sot's small-minded blathering," Nicolette blurted, digging her heels in, forcing him to stop and face her. "I'm begging you. Please. Don't go through with this."

Blowing out a long breath, he lay his hand atop hers, resting in the crook of his arm. "He cannot speak so disparagingly of you, Nicolette, and not be held accountable."

Tears clogged her throat at his inflexible defense of her. But as much as she appreciated it, the stark reality was, how she felt about herself was what mattered. Not what others thought of her.

She'd spent two long years, trying to prove to *le beau monde* she didn't care about their opinions. And it wasn't until this moment, when faced with a choice between her reputation and Mathias's safety, that the truth convicted her.

None of them mattered a jot. *He* did.

"What if…? What if he apologizes?" she asked.

Would Kilbourne?

"Would…would that suffice?"

"It's done, my love." Mathias tenderly touched her cheek. "Come, I need to find Sutcliffe and Pennington, and you should go home at once. I'm sure in a matter of minutes, despite my threat, the guests will be abuzz with the news."

At the top of the terrace stairs, Nicolette slowed her steps once more and summoning every jot of courage she possessed, asked. "Mathias, do you love me?"

He turned, incredulity darkening his eyes to midnight blue. Gold flecks glinted in his irises, and her heart swelled with what she saw there. Cupping her cheek in his palm, he rested his forehead against hers.

"How can you doubt it, my darling? I've been unable to keep my eyes off you for two very long years. But I knew you needed time to find your own way, and I prayed, daily, that it would lead you to me."

Tenderly cupping her cheeks, he kissed her forehead.

"Then, I beg you, don't do this." Nicolette clutched his hand and held it to her chest over her heart with both of hers. "I love you, too. I do, so, *so* much. I never thought to find this kind of love."

He flashed her a blinding smile and crushed her to him. "Thank God," he whispered into her hair, his voice thick and raspy with suppressed emotion.

Her head tucked beneath his chin, and her face pressed to his chest, she absorbed his heat and his masculine essence.

"I love you, Nicolette. Love your spirit and wit, your laughter and sarcasm, your winsome smile, and your magnificent eyes. I think I fell in love with you the first time I looked into your beautiful eyes."

He had?

Why hadn't he said anything all this time?

Ah, because Kilbourne had been courting her and had become her affianced shortly thereafter. And being the honorable man that he was, Mathias would never declare himself to a woman another had claimed. Then after she'd been discarded, she'd been rather a horror to men in general.

"I love you, Nicolette."

His words were a balm, filling her with contentment and peace. Much like burrowing beneath thick layers of bedding during a spring storm. Sighing, she snuggled closer, permitting her eyelids to flutter shut. Loving him so much, her heart so full to bursting, it almost hurt.

"Our love means more to me than *anything* else, Mathias. Anything."

"For me as well, darling."

Angling her head, Nicolette grazed her fingertips over his granite-like jaw.

"If I can ignore Kilbourne's insults, can you not also? For me? I..." She swallowed against the torrent of emotion, besetting her. "I don't think I could go on without you, Mathias."

Her voice broke, and she had to take a moment to compose herself.

"You are my other half," she said. "I am not complete without you. *Please*. We've only just acknowledged our love for each other. I want to explore this beautiful thing between us and watch it grow and bloom."

His eyes a firestorm of emotion, Mathias stared into hers for so long, his cheekbones standing out starkly in his classically sculpted face, that she considered he might not respond. That she'd asked too much of him.

"How can I deny you, my heart?" Mathias released a juddery sigh, one large hand brushing up and down her spine. "At least let me knock him senseless at Gentleman Jack's. My manly pride demands he sport a black eye and a bruised face for what he said about you."

"Yes. *Yes.*" Tears cascaded over Nicolette's cheeks as she stood on her toes and peppered his beloved face with desperate kisses. She gave a watery laugh. "Yes. That will do. Blacken both his eyes if you wish and break his nose, too. He has an entirely too high opinion of himself."

"I must tell you something, Nicolette. Something my sister isn't even aware of. It can never, *never* become known." He firmed his mouth into a grim line. "I would have no secrets between us."

She tilted her head and searched his face. "You can tell me anything, Mathias, and I would never breathe a word."

His eyes softened, and he caressed her cheek with his fingertip. His voice low, he murmured for her ears alone, "My mother was set upon mere days before my parents married. I was born eight- and one-half months later. My mother neither knows who her assailant was, nor for certain who my father is."

"Oh, Mathias." Her gorgeous eyes grew luminous. "Your poor mother."

He tilted his mouth into a poignant half-smile. "My father adored her, and they were very happy. He always treated me as his own, even though he never knew whether I was or not."

"Thank you for trusting me with something so private, Mathias. Rest assured, I will never even let your mother know I'm aware."

"Thank you." He kissed her nose. "I could not in good conscience take you as my wife, Nicolette, without confiding in you."

"It makes no difference to me who sired you." She

pressed a kiss to his hand. "It's *you I* love."

"*Mathias*!" Lady Calbraith's plaintive wail cut through the peaceful night. "Oh, Mathias, my dearest, tell me it isn't so."

One arm draped around Nicolette's waist, he turned to face the viscountess as she glided across the terrace, her features arranged in carefully contrived distress. Her gown hugged her voluptuous curves, accenting her shapely figure to perfection. And as was her wont, her bountiful breasts were on full display, bouncing gently as she rushed toward them.

"*What* isn't so?" He traced his fingers up and down Nicolette's bare arm. "That I called Kilbourne out for insulting my betrothed? Or that I am to wed the most marvelous woman in the world?"

Other guests began trailing onto the terrace, whether to see what the commotion was about or whether they'd heard the news of the pending duel, Nicolette couldn't guess.

Or...had Kilbourne wasted no time in sullying her reputation?

She realized with a start, she really and honestly

didn't give a bloody damn.

Mathias loved her, and she loved him. Everything else was inconsequential.

Lady Calbraith blinked several times, her mouth opening and closing like a freshly caught salmon. Or that peculiar little monkey Nicolette had seen once at the fair.

"*What?*" The viscountess managed, at last, her voice very much sounding like she'd gargled shards of glass. "*M...m...marry?*"

She said the word as if enunciating an obscene oath.

Nicolette couldn't prevent the small, jubilant smile curving her mouth.

Well, perhaps, *not* so very small.

At least two dozen guests crowded near them now, including her Mother, the Sutcliffes, Rayne, Gabriella and Ophelia, and those bruising Scottish dukes.

"Whatever is going on?" Everleigh asked, sweeping to the front of the engrossed crowd, white lines bracketing her mouth.

A wide grin splitting his handsome face, Mathias

dropped to one knee before Nicolette. "I'm proposing to the most remarkable, intriguing woman."

"*Oh, my*," Everleigh breathed with approval. She cast a beaming smile to her husband and reached for his hand. "Isn't it the most romantic thing, Griffin?"

"Indeed," came the duke's droll response.

Several delighted feminine gasps echoed—and perhaps a few not so very thrilled, as well.

"I knew it!" Nicolette clearly heard Ophelia exclaim. "Didn't I tell you, Gabby and Rayne? Oh, this is simply marvelous."

A familiar male figure edged forward, and head canted, he crossed his arms.

Ansley?

His penetrating gaze drifting between her and Mathias, and a reserved smile slanting his mouth, he gave an approving nod.

Joy warmed Nicolette's veins as she returned her attention to Mathias, though her vision was decidedly blurry and her smile tremulous.

He took both her hands in his and gazed into her eyes with such earnestness, her breath caught. It seemed to do that quite often in his presence.

"Oh, my goodness," she heard Mama say amidst sniffles. "I'm so delighted."

A hush settled over the crowd, anticipation fairly vibrating in the air.

"Nicolette Adelia Estelle Twistleton, I adore you. I want to spend every day of the rest of my life, looking into your glorious eyes and putting a smile on your face." Mathias winked naughtily. "And perhaps even ride elephants together in Africa and Asia."

A tear slipped unbidden from the corner of one of her eyes.

"And maybe camels," she managed to mutter. "The ones with two humps."

"Anything you wish." He pressed his mouth to the knuckles of each of her hands in turn. "Will you marry me, darling?"

"How can I possibly say no?" She blinked to clear the moisture from her eyes. "I love you."

"Nooo!" A woman's distressed cry echoed into the still night. "You cannot marry *her*."

"Indeed, he can, Lady Calbraith," Ansley said

briskly. "Might I suggest now would be an excellent time for you to depart?"

Footsteps rapidly retreating, followed the viscountess's angry huff.

Mathias regained his feet, and in full view of her brother, mother, and at least fifty of London's most elite peers and peeresses, he kissed Nicolette soundly.

Most soundly, indeed.

"Can I assume that is a yes, my love?" he asked amidst scandalous applause and several "Huzzahs!"

"You can, my darling." Shaking her head, Nicolette chuckled as she fingered his lapel. "I'm ever so glad I agreed to dance with a duke, after all."

"As am I." Mathias lowered his head again. "As am I."

Epilogue

East India Docks
London England
28 June 1810

Mathias tossed his hat on the table beneath the circular window in the ship's cabin that would be his and Nicolette's home for the next few weeks. Two traveling trunks had been placed at the end of the berth, and another pair had been arranged on the opposite wall beneath the porthole.

He and his wife of three splendid days were on their way to ride elephants in Asia. Excursions in Greece, Morocco, Italy, and Spain were also on the itinerary.

Nicolette had wanted to add several other locations to their travels, but he couldn't be away from his business ventures or his ducal responsibilities that long. Instead, he'd promised her another extended trip next year.

His duchess possessed quite an adventurous nature, both in *and* out of the bedchamber.

She removed her ivory and peach bonnet and her apricot-colored spencer and slowly turned in a circle. "I don't know why, but I'd always imagined ship's cabins were much larger than this."

Mathias had no complaints. The smaller the cabin, the closer she'd be to him, although that bed might prove a bit crowded.

Giving him a saucy grin, she crossed the short distance and twined her arms about his neck, asking coyly, "Do you suppose we'll grow tired of one another's company by the time we arrive in Calcutta?"

"Hmm." Wrapping his arms around her waist, he grinned and leaned back to peruse her beautiful face. "I *suppose* I could read a few of those books you insisted upon bringing. But I think we'll be too busy, '*exploring this beautiful thing between us and watching it grow.*'"

His grin taking in a seductive bend at the double entendre, he arched his hardened member into her soft stomach.

"Ah, throwing my words back at me already, husband?" She reached between them, grazing her hand over his hardness, a siren's promise in her sultry blue eyes.

"Hmm, mayhap." He skimmed her muslin gown upward, exposing her shapely silk, stocking-clad legs and half-boots. Peach and coral roses adorned her stockings today.

"Mathias," she breathed on a husky rasp as he backed her up against the bulkhead. "We haven't even left port yet."

"Ah, but I believe you told me you wanted more adventure in your life." He flashed a sinfully, wicked smile as his fingers grazed her bare hips. "I do so like the current fashion of no undergarments."

"Oh, I had several pairs of pantalettes made—"

"Which you will *not* wear unless we are in Siberia

or Antarctica," he said before nuzzling her neck. "I shouldn't like unnecessary obstacles to curtail our explorations."

As he murmured against her fragrant, satiny throat, he cupped her deliciously rounded buttocks.

Nicolette possessed the most delectably formed bottom he'd ever seen.

"Mathias," she gasped, arching into him, one hand clutching at his shoulders and the other working at the falls of his pantaloons.

He growled low in his throat, every ounce of blood in his body, shooting straight to his cock. "Minx."

He slipped a finger along her sex, gratified to feel her slick and ready for him.

"I should be the one complaining." Nicolette freed his swollen manhood from his constraints and wrapped her small, warm hand around its length. "*You* always have an obstacle to *my* explorations."

He gritted his teeth, the exquisite pleasure so intense, he was in danger of spilling in her hand. Grasping her waist, he lifted her, grating out, "Wrap your legs around my waist and your arms around my neck."

"Oh, my," she whispered as she complied. "This is certainly adventuresome."

Holding her against the cabin wall, he angled his pelvis and found the hot entrance to her sex.

"Hurry, Mathias." She wiggled her hips, as eager for their union as he was. "I want you inside me."

"As you wish, my love." He slid into her, closing his eyes as her tight channel contracted around him. "God, Nicolette," he groaned before capturing her mouth in a ravenous kiss.

Mimicking the thrusting of his hips with the plunging of his tongue, he took her hard and fast, encouraged as she met him stroke for stroke.

Her whimpers grew into little mewls until she was digging her nails into his shoulders. Tearing her mouth from his, she buried her head into the crook of his neck, keening softly as her body shuddered over and over.

Feeling her come undone around him, catapulted him over the precipice, and he pounded into her, his seed spilling from his body in hot spurts. "Nicolette, love," he rasped hoarsely.

Breathing heavily, Mathias cradled her until her ragged breathing returned to normal and then gently lowered her legs to the floor.

She wobbled and giggled as her skirts settled about her feet once more. "Well, that was quite...*educational*."

"I intend to see that you have a very, very thorough education." He kissed her tenderly. "Shall we go atop and watch as the ship puts to sea?" he asked, casting a glance out the porthole.

"No, I think we should continue my education."

"You do, do you?" Cocking an eyebrow, he grasped her waist, his member already stirring to life again. "Did you have any particular lesson you wished to learn?"

"I saw a stallion mount a mare from behind once." She wrapped a finger in his neckcloth. "We haven't tried that position yet."

Sweet Jesus, she'd be the death of him.

"Well, never let it be said that I didn't gratify my delectable wife's curiosity."

And he did, most satisfactorily.

About the Author

USA Today Bestselling, award-winning author COLLETTE CAMERON® scribbles Scottish and Regency historicals featuring dashing rogues and scoundrels and the intrepid damsels who reform them.Blessed with an overactive and witty muse that won't stop whispering new romantic romps in her ear, she's lived in Oregon her entire life, though she dreams of living in Scotland part-time. A self-confessed Cadbury chocoholic, you'll always find a dash of inspiration and a pinch of humor in her sweet-to-spicy timeless romances®.

Explore **Collette's worlds** at
www.collettecameron.com!

Join her **VIP Reader Club** and **FREE newsletter**.
Giggles guaranteed!

FREE BOOK: Join Collette's The Regency Rose® VIP Reader Club to get updates on book releases, cover reveals, contests, and giveaways she reserves exclusively for email and newsletter followers. Also, any deals, sales, or special promotions are offered to club members first. She will not share your name or email, nor will she spam you.

http://bit.ly/TheRegencyRoseGift

Dearest Reader,

Thank you for reading NEVER DANCE WITH A DUKE.

Nicolette Twistleton has appeared on the pages of several of my SEDUCTIVE SCOUNDRELS SERIES, and I wanted readers to empathize with her, but also appreciate her independent spirit. She needed an understanding hero, who would give her room to be herself but was there to support and defend her.

Mathias was the perfect hero for her. He waited patiently for her to heal and offered her friendship and taught her to trust men again. I really adore him!

Watch for HOW TO WIN A DUKE'S HEART, Sophronie Slater and Evan Gordonstone, Duke of Waycross's story and THE DEBUTANTE AND THE DUKE, Rayne Wellbrook and Fletcher McQuinton, Duke of Kincade, romances coming soon.

Please consider telling other readers why you enjoyed this book by reviewing it. I adore hearing from my readers.

Here's wishing you many happy hours of reading, more happily-ever-afters than you can possibly enjoy in a lifetime, and abundant blessings to you and your loved ones.

Collette Cameron

A Diamond for a Duke

Seductive Scoundrels Series Book One
A Historical Regency Romance

A dour duke. A wistful wallflower. An impossible match.

Jules, Sixth Duke of Dandridge, disdains Society and all its trappings, preferring the country's solitude and peace. Already jaded after the woman he loved died years ago, he's become even more so since unexpectedly inheriting a dukedom's responsibilities and finding himself the target of every husband-hunting vixen and matchmaker mother in London.

Jemmah Dament has adored Jules from afar for years—since before her family's financial and social reversals. She dares not dream she can win a duke's heart any more than she hopes to escape the life of servitude imposed on her by an uncaring mother. Jemmah knows full well Jules is too far above her station now. Besides, his family has already selected his perfect duchess: a poised, polished, exquisite blueblood.

A chance encounter reunites Jules and Jemmah, resulting in a passionate interlude neither can forget. Jules realizes he wants more—much more—than Jemmah's sweet kisses or her warming his bed. He must somehow convince her to gamble on a dour duke. But can Jemmah trust a man promised to another? One who's sworn never to love again?

Duchess Of His Heart

Seductive Scoundrels Series Book Six
A Historical Regency Romance

He once loved her beyond all reason. Dare he risk heartbreak again?

Leaving her first love behind was the hardest thing Regine, Duchess of Heartwaite, had ever done. Her marriage of convenience to another man saved her family, even as it laid waste to her heart. That was years ago, however. Now widowed, she's ready to begin her life anew. But all it takes is one glimpse of her former sweetheart to realize the feelings she buried so long ago are still there, stronger than ever. Unfortunately, his feelings for her are decidedly colder…

Solicitor James Brentwood has only one mistress these days—his work. Being jilted by his betrothed taught him love simply wasn't worth the cost. But Regine is back in England now, more beautiful and alluring than ever. And it's not long before he begins to feel things he has no business feeling. Especially not for her. Not again.

But when a nemesis intent on destroying Regine emerges, it's James who must come to her rescue. Can they overcome their differences and painful past to claim their happily ever after? Or will their second chance at love end as disastrously as their first?

Prologue

Duchess Of His Heart

Seductive Scoundrels Series Book Six

1

Colchester, England

September 1802

Standing in the apple orchard, a short walking distance from the village of Colchester and All Saint's Priory—his father's parish—James Brentwood gazed overhead. Ribbons of sunlight threaded through the thick, verdant foliage heavily laden with crisp, crimson fruit.

Closing his eyes, he inhaled the familiar scents from his childhood: rich, warm earth, ripe apples, freshly cut hay, and an occasional whiff of honeysuckle drifting by on the capricious fall breeze.

Nearby, industrious bees hummed as they went about their work, and songbirds trilled while flitting from branch to branch. In the distance, his sister's chickens cackled, and a horse neighed in the adjacent pasture. He missed the peace and freshness of the English countryside when in London.

Before letting his mind wander once more, he cast a puzzled glance down the dusty, rutted lane. Regine was several minutes late. Unusual for her. Typically, she was as eager for their clandestine meetings as he, and she often beat him to their rendezvous.

Regine. Just thinking of his beloved tightened James's chest as overwhelming emotion tunneled through his veins. God, how he loved her. Since she'd been a toddler and he a young lad, he'd adored the raven-haired beauty with eyes so blue, they put the summer sky to shame.

If not for her father's recent and unexpected death,

he would've asked for her hand in marriage this visit even though two years of his solicitor's training remained. He'd have to bide his time a jot longer, blast it all.

Scratching his temple, he grinned with unchecked happiness. Regine had agreed to become his wife over a year ago. They kept the agreement a secret but often spoke of their future residing together in London—him a successful solicitor and she, the mother of his four— *no five*—children.

Neither aspired to wealth or position nor coveted possessions. Each only needed the other, and they would be happy and content for the rest of their lives. Or so they'd vowed between passionate kisses and promises of eternal love.

Tomorrow, he'd return to London, but he'd savor these last few hours with Regine before bidding her farewell—after tasting her sweet mouth and breathing in her apple and spices fragrance one final time. Finances wouldn't permit him to return for at least a fortnight, and he craved memories to savor until her lush form was wrapped in his embrace once more.

At last, he heard muffled footsteps approaching, and he turned, excitement and expectation vying for supremacy. At eighteen, Regine Edenshaw was a vision, even in her somber, black gown. Her unbound silky, ebony hair swayed as she walked, her eyes downcast and neck bent as if deep in thought.

She was his. *His.* Or would be as soon as her mourning period ended. James would have to harness his impatience for a few more months before asking Mrs. Edenshaw for her daughter's hand. Pray God Regine's mother wouldn't require them to wait an entire year to wed as mourning protocol dictated.

Regine stopped a few feet away and reluctantly brought her gaze up to meet his.

His heart stalled at the intense sorrow and regret pooled in her eyes. Eyes sparkling with unshed tears.

Her lips parted, but no words came forth.

"Darling, what is it?" He moved to gather her into his arms, to soothe away whatever had distressed her, but she shook her head and held a palm up to ward him off. Torment ravaged her delicate features.

Alarm took root, spiraling outward from James's

stomach and sending a chill washing over him. By God, if someone had dared to harm her.

"Sweetheart?" He brushed a fingertip across her satiny cheek. "What has you so distressed? Tell me." Somehow, he'd make whatever troubled her right— anything to put a smile on her bowed mouth and erase the sadness shadowing her azure eyes.

"James…" Shoulders slumping, she clamped her lower lip between her teeth, and her lashes fluttered downward to caress her pale cheeks.

His trepidation kicked up several notches, and dread engulfed him. The instinct that made him a damn good solicitor fairly shrieked. He wasn't going to like what she said. Not at all.

"James," she murmured again, her voice a mere thread of sound—a soft, spine-tingling entreaty in the now eerily silent orchard. Then she opened her mouth, gulped in a deep breath, and thrust her chin upward as if bracing herself.

Against what, for God's sake?

He swept the area with a swift, apprehensive glance, before settling his attention uneasily upon her once more. Something akin to terror knotted in his throat at the defeat and devastation he detected in her startlingly blue eyes. It stripped the air from his lungs and squeezed his heart in a ruthless, unyielding vise.

"I...," she drew in a ragged breath. "I am to be married," she finally said in a rush, dropping her focus to her hands, repeatedly wadding her black skirts.

What? Married? No. No. You're mine. Mine! My dearest, most precious love.

"Pardon?" he whispered stupidly, his lips stiff and voice gravelly with disbelief and pain. "Married?" He shook his head. He couldn't have heard her correctly. But he had. Her tense posture and waxen pallor revealed the truth.

"To who?" Or was it whom? What the hell did it matter? His thoughts raced, pell-mell, around his befuddled mind, all ability to reason calmly having flown. *You cannot marry another. You cannot! You said you'd be my wife.*

"To the Duke of Heartwaite," she replied, her voice flat and devoid of emotion.

A bloody duke? He fisted his hands until the nails cut deeply into his palms.

How could he, a poor vicar's son with scarcely two coins to rub together and in training to become a solicitor, compete with a sodding duke? Moisture blurring his vision, he choked out a single, strangled syllable, "When?"

"Next week." Her throat working and her hand trembling, she touched a bent knuckle to the corner of one eye. "I'm so sorry, James."

"Why?" He tenderly grasped her slender arms, peering into her anguished eyes awash with tears. "Why, Regine? I love you. You love me, too." Didn't she? Yes, else why would she be this miserable? "Please, I beg you, don't do this to us."

Eyes wide and tortured, she silently gazed at him, and the truth slammed into James with the force of an over-loaded grain wagon. A duke could offer her everything he couldn't: position, power, prestige, and wealth.

Evidently, love was a trifling insignificance

compared to those *necessities*.

James stumbled backward, shaking his head, the pain eviscerating him so excruciating, he almost doubled over. Almost roared aloud against the knives carving and cleaving unmercifully into his heart and soul. And he did what any animal mortally wounded did. Reacted with primal rage and the urge to protect itself.

Curling his upper lip into a sneer, he raked his contemptuous gaze over her. "I've been so damned stupid." A complete and utter idiot. "I believed you were different. That money and position didn't matter—"

"They don't, James. Not in the way you think." She held a delicate palm out to him, beseechingly. "Please let me explain. I owe you that much." Her voice broke, and when he didn't take her outstretched hand, she let it drop to her side. "I am sorry," she murmured again, her face ashen, and her eyes wounded pools.

Sorry? *Sorry?* He didn't want her God-damned

apology. He wanted her!

Something inside him splintered, fracturing into a million pieces, and where his heart had once been, an unfeeling stone replaced the mangled organ.

He threw his head back and laughed, harsh and cynical. "*You* don't owe *me* anything, Regine." With that, he turned his back and stalked away, resolutely disregarding her sobs, her vows that she loved him, and her pleas for him to listen to her.

Never again would he be taken in by a beautiful face or pledges of love and promises of forever.

Printed in Great Britain
by Amazon

68048401R00119